"Cara, we can court an[...] I—I don't want to rush you."

"Danke, Matthew." She was touched. "But like you, it's a little late in life for me to find a *hutband*. I think we can plan a wedding in three months."

"Ja gut."

At the genuine smile of joy on his face, Cara felt the punch of guilt in her gut. November was the traditional month Amish couples got married, and she had planned this trip with that possibility in mind.

And if he chose to discard her—not that she would blame him—then she had the backup plan of working in the town's start-up cannery.

"Danke, Matthew. I'll be down in the morning."

He took the hint and departed. She closed the door behind him, then leaned against it and shut her eyes. *"Danke, Gott,"* she whispered. The first meeting had gone well.

But she knew she couldn't hide her secret forever.

Living on a remote self-sufficient homestead in North Idaho, **Patrice Lewis** is a Christian wife, mother, author, blogger, columnist and speaker. She has practiced and written about rural subjects for almost thirty years. When she isn't writing, Patrice enjoys self-sufficiency projects, such as animal husbandry, small-scale dairy production, gardening, food preservation and canning, and homeschooling. She and her husband have been married since 1990 and have two daughters.

Books by Patrice Lewis

Love Inspired

The Amish Newcomer
Amish Baby Lessons
Her Path to Redemption
The Amish Animal Doctor
The Mysterious Amish Nanny
Their Road to Redemption
The Amish Midwife's Bargain
The Amish Beekeeper's Dilemma
Uncovering Her Amish Past
The Amish Bride's Secret

Visit the Author Profile page at LoveInspired.com.

He that is without sin among you,
let him first cast a stone at her.
—*John* 8:7

To my husband and daughters,
my greatest earthly joy.

To Jesus, for His redeeming grace.

To God, who has blessed me
more than I could possibly deserve.

Chapter One

Cara Lengacher stopped in front of the large, square three-story building. A sign on the street side proclaimed it was Miller's Boardinghouse. This, she hoped, would be her new home. A little voice inside her asked, what had she gotten herself into?

She had never traveled much, certainly had never been west of the Mississippi. Yet here she was, about to embark upon the adventure of a lifetime.

The last few days were a blur. Her angry father. Her mother, weeping. A taxi ride to the airport. A flight across the country. A bus ride to the tiny town of Pierce, Montana, located on the mountainous western side of the state.

But rather than being met by the man who might become her *hutband*, there was no one waiting for her at the bus stop at all. Cara couldn't blame the man. The bus had pulled into town an hour earlier than scheduled. Without any options, Cara had set out in search of her new home—and new husband.

She knew the town of Pierce was small—about 3,500 people—and isolated. She just didn't expect it to be *this* isolated. The bus had passed other small towns at distant intervals, but nothing that could remotely be called a city. Instead, she saw forests and fields, while the western horizon was dominated by the high peaks of craggy mountains. The September landscape had a tired look, but aspens were turning color and she could see early signs of the changing seasons.

But walking through the town on her way to find the boardinghouse, she was impressed. The community looked snug and welcoming. Whether the man waiting for her at the boardinghouse would be equally welcoming...well, all she could do was pray.

Now that the moment was here, she pressed a hand to her midsection. Then she lifted her chin, touched her *kapp* to make sure it was straight, and entered the building.

The lobby was empty. She looked around. It was a typical Plain establishment of clean lines, lots of wood, and scrupulously clean and simple furnishings. A check-in counter stood in one corner, with a closed door behind it. On the surface was a desk bell. She tapped it smartly, then stood quiet, heart beating fast.

Within a few moments, the door opened and a man stepped out. He eyed her *kapp* and spoke in Deutsch. "May I help you?"

"Are you Matthew Miller?"

"*Ja.*"

"I'm Cara Lengacher."

His eyes widened with a comical mixture of excitement and alarm. "But your bus... I was supposed to pick you up... you're early!"

Cara hadn't known what to expect from her future *hutband*. Certainly she didn't expect him to be as good-looking as he was: dark blue eyes with laugh lines at the corners, straight brown hair cut short. He was lean and seemed good-humored. She breathed a sigh of relief and offered her most brilliant smile. "*Ja*, the bus was about an hour earlier than scheduled. I had no way to reach you, so I walked here from the bus stop. It's a *gut* thing the town is so small!"

He came from behind the counter through a pass-through gate and held out a hand. "I'm so glad you're here." She placed her hand in his. He held it a touch longer than convention dictated, but then again—with *Gott's* help—they would be married in less than three months. And if they weren't...at least she had a promised job to fall back upon.

Finally he dropped her hand. "What about your luggage?"

"It's stored in some lockers at the bus stop. I have four large suitcases. It's rather a lot, I know, but—"

"But hopefully you'll be here a long time." He grinned. "Let me hitch up the horse and we'll go get them."

Cara trailed after him to an outdoor courtyard with a buggy covered by an awning and an adjacent stable for the horse. She watched as he hitched up the animal with efficient movements. Soon enough he was courteously assisting her into the buggy. He clucked to the horse.

"I can't apologize enough for not being at the bus stop when you arrived," he said, guiding the animal down a side street toward the edge of town. "I planned to be there well in advance of five o'clock, I can assure you."

"It's not your fault," she told him, and couldn't suppress a small sigh of fatigue. "I'm just glad to be here at last."

"I've set aside the nicest room in the boardinghouse for you," he continued. He stopped the horse at an intersection, then continued down the street. "The place you'll be working is Yoder's Mercantile, which is on Main Street about three blocks away from the boardinghouse. The Yoders have purchased a smaller building right next to their main store, and that's where they're putting in the community cannery."

"That will be my territory," she said. She made sure her voice was cheerful. "I've always loved canning, and now I can earn my living doing so. What are the Yoders like? Abe and Mabel, *ja*?"

"*Ja.* They're a middle-aged couple and just about two of the nicest people you'll ever meet. They were excited to have someone with your qualifications overseeing the opening and running of the cannery."

"When will it be ready to open?"

"It should be ready now, *Gott* willing. I've been working on its construction as the main carpenter, since I live so close. It's not hard to split my time between that and running the boardinghouse. The cannery is a large space, probably way larger than you need at the moment."

Cara smiled. "The cannery where I worked in Pennsylvania was huge. We put out over a hundred recipes and shipped all over the country. I'm excited about starting a smaller cannery from the ground up. I brought a lot of reference books and USDA-approved recipes."

Matthew directed the horse back onto the main street and pulled the animal to a stop at the crossing of the rural, two-lane highway that skirted the edge of town. When traffic was clear, he clucked to the horse, crossed the highway and entered the parking lot of the bus stop.

"There are the lockers." Cara pointed.

Matthew pulled the horse to a stop in front of the bank of roomy lockers. Cara climbed out of the buggy, entered a code on the keypad and withdrew her suitcases one by one. Matthew stowed them in the back of the buggy. Within a few moments they were heading back across the highway.

"Most of the time I take the back streets to avoid car traffic," he said, "but we'll go back on Main Street so I can point out some of the sights."

"*Ja gut.* I liked what I saw when I walked. Pierce seems like a nice little town."

"It is, and the townspeople have been very welcoming to us since the church bought a huge ranch on the outskirts. The Amish settlement is on the other side of town, about three miles beyond the boundary. The settlement itself is not a town, just a collection of farms. We all come into Pierce whenever we need to do business. Look." He pointed. "That's Yoder's Mercantile. And the building to the left is the cannery."

"Right on Main Street. Lots of exposure." Cara looked at the buildings with assessing eyes. "This seems like a bustling little town, for all it's so small."

"We're the county seat, and because it's so isolated, it has just about everything necessary." He started ticking off on his fingers. "Two grocery stores, a small hospital, a home furnishings store, several thrift stores, all the county services you'd expect."

"And a lovely park." She pointed ahead.

"*Ja*, but we turn off here." Matthew directed the horse to the right down a side street.

Cara eyed the three-story building as it came into view. "The boardinghouse is a handsome structure."

"*Ja*, my parents had a *gut* eye when they bought it. It took some time to renovate, but we've been open four years now. It's become something of a catch-all business. We rent rooms, of course, and often *Englischers* treat it as a kind of motel. We've hosted a few church weddings too."

Cara wanted to ask about his financial status, but it seemed rude to inquire so soon into their acquaintance. Instead she asked, "How many women answered your ad?"

"Just one."

Cara blushed but remained silent.

Matthew pulled the horse into a courtyard and climbed out of the buggy. "Give me a moment. I'll grab the luggage cart in the building."

She lingered by the side of the buggy, enjoying the cozy feeling of the bricked courtyard with a generous oak tree shading one corner.

Matthew rolled out the cart, and she helped him load her suitcases onto it. After he unhitched and stabled the horse, she followed him indoors. He carried the two heaviest suitcases up the stairs. She followed with the two lighter ones. He shouldered open the door to a bright room with the evening sun shining through the leaves of the large maple tree outside.

She stopped and stared. "This is lovely."

"Danke." He put the suitcases on the floor and lingered awkwardly for a moment. She saw a blush creep up his face. "Cara, just so you know, if you're not comfortable getting married by November, we can court another year. I—I don't want to rush you."

"Danke, Matthew." She was touched. "But like you, I'm twenty-six. It's a little late in life for me to find a *hutband.* I think we can plan a wedding in three months."

"Ja gut."

At the genuine smile of joy on his face, she felt the punch of guilt in her gut. November was the traditional month Amish couples got married, and she had planned this trip with that possibility in mind.

And if he chose to discard her—not that she would blame him—then she had the backup plan of working in the town's startup cannery. She wondered how hard it would be to find another place to live, if need be.

But she was away from her father. Right now, that was what mattered most.

"I'll leave you to unpack, then." Matthew lingered in the door for a moment. "Have you eaten?"

"Actually, *ja*. I'll be fine for the evening." Right now she just needed to be alone for a while. "You don't provide meals here, do you?"

"*Nein*, just rooms. But since my living quarters are downstairs behind the front desk, you're welcome to use the kitchen." He grinned. "I'm not the world's greatest cook, but I make a *gut* omelet."

"That sounds *gut*. *Danke*, Matthew. I'll see you in the morning."

He took the hint and departed. Closing the door behind him, she leaned against it and shut her eyes. *"Danke, Gott,"* she whispered. Their first meeting had gone well.

But she knew she couldn't hide her secret forever. At some point before November, she would have to tell Matthew that she carried another man's child.

Matthew descended the stairs to the lobby grinning from ear to ear. He couldn't believe his carefully worded ad in *The Budget* had produced such incredible results.

If Cara was as she seemed—and he saw no reason to doubt it—she would make a wonderful wife. She was far prettier than he anticipated—tall, willowy, with melting dark eyes and dark blond hair, and a smile that could knock a man flat at ten paces. Even her voice was silvery—sweet and pleasant.

She'd told him in her letters that her

fiancé had abandoned her for another woman, leaving her reputation in tatters. And that her parents blamed her for the man's desertion. Desperate to get away from her home town in Pennsylvania, she'd admitted that moving to the other side of the country held a lot of appeal.

Whatever her reasons, he was glad she was here at last. It seemed that after years of hoping, and one failed attempt to lure a woman from his old Ohio church out here, *Gott* had provided him with a woman who could become his wife.

Granted, his method was a bit unorthodox. He'd heard of people advertising for a wife, but it wasn't common nowadays. His parents disapproved of it—bitterly— but in his mind, success was success.

He understood what Cara had been through when she was dumped by the man who was courting her. He himself had been thrown over by the woman he was courting long-distance. There was a shortage of marriageable women in this new Amish settlement, and he wasn't the first to bring a bride from back east. But in the end, his remote courtship had failed when the woman decided she didn't want to live so far away from her family.

Increasingly lonely, he thought advertising for a wife might work. And *Gott* had provided.

He practically danced his way down the stairs and into his private quarters behind the front desk. He stopped on the threshold and tried to see it from a stranger's perspective. Would she be happy living here?

The living space was generous: three bedrooms, a large kitchen with a big dining table, a good-sized living room. Surely there was enough space for a wife. And, someday—*Gott* willing—maybe a *boppli*. After that, he could claim some of the rental rooms on the ground floor for his own. The building was vast. It could easily absorb a large family while he still rented out rooms to people.

His joy was too big to contain. He had to tell someone. He snatched his straw hat, plopped it on his head and headed three blocks down the street to Yoder's Mercantile.

Inside, Abe and Mabel Yoder were just in the process of closing the store for the evening. Their younger bookkeeper, Thomas Kemp, was bent over some paperwork next to Abe.

"She's here!" he announced the moment he stepped foot inside the store.

They jerked their heads up and stared at him.

"Who's here?" Mabel asked, her hands suspended midair as she paused cleaning tables and chairs in the café area.

"Cara! She's just arrived!" He could feel his grin split his face.

"Your bride?" A smile wreathed Mabel's face. "Why didn't you say so! What's she like?"

"Almost too *gut* to be true." Matthew pumped a fist, trying to contain his giddiness. "She's much prettier than I thought. She seems like a kind woman. She has a beautiful smile. You'll all meet her tomorrow, of course. But I—I—"

Abe Yoder chuckled. "Calm down, young man."

"It's hard. I've waited so long. I guess I can't believe she's actually here."

Thomas Kemp laughed. "I've been married now for almost three years, and I still feel the same way about *my* bride."

Matthew grinned at the other man, who was about his age. "Then you understand."

Mabel gave a final swipe to a tabletop. "Well, I'm looking forward to meeting her and getting the cannery up and running."

"Speaking of which…" Matthew put aside his personal feelings with some effort. People in the church weren't usually so demonstrative about their emotions, and he knew his outburst probably caused some feelings of awkwardness among the others. "Abe, you mentioned something the other day about a plan for the rest of the cannery building. What was that about?"

The older man chuckled. "If you don't remember, I think it's because you had your head in the clouds."

"*Ja*, maybe."

"*Komm* with me and I'll *show* you, not just *tell* you again."

Matthew followed the store owner through the connecting door that led into the smaller building next door.

The space was small by retail standards, perhaps 2,000 square feet. The Yoders' idea to purchase the building and turn it into a community cannery for church members was an exciting one. Matthew was pleased they had asked him to do the renovations, since the work could be done on his own schedule. The extra income he was earning was being put away for his upcoming marriage.

But only half the space—the back end

of the building—was being used for the cannery. The front half was undetermined and unfinished, with bare stud walls and exposed infrastructure. There was a door that led directly to the street and was always locked, though Matthew possessed the key in case he needed to do anything after the mercantile was closed for the evening.

"See this?" Abe pointed out the newly installed, large stainless steel industrial workspaces of the cannery. "I don't expect the cannery will need much more room to expand, so Mabel and I had an idea to use the other half of the building to put in an in-house bakery to provide the store with its own selection of fresh breads, and maybe pies and cookies and such."

Matthew whistled. "What a *gut* idea! I know Esther Mast already supplies you with pastries, but you haven't been carrying bread except for the occasional artisanal loaf. Do you want me to do the carpentry to build it?"

"If you have the time, *ja*."

"I do, *ja*." Matthew was pleased with the offer of extra work.

"Also…" Abe looked down at the floor for a moment, then raised his head and met Matthew's eyes. "I know your parents aren't too happy with the thought of you advertising for a wife. Since they're the actual owners of the boardinghouse, I'm aware there's a chance you could lose both your job and your living quarters. Mabel and I want you to know that if something happens and the boarding- house job dries up, you'll always have a position at the store."

Matthew's eyes suddenly stung. His parents' disapproval of his method of finding a wife was a heavier burden than he expected. He had always gotten along so well with his *mamm* and *daed* that their displeasure was difficult to face.

Into the brief silence, while Matthew

worked to master his emotions, Abe continued. "There's another thing. Should you suddenly find yourself without a place to live…well, it wouldn't take much to turn this space into something livable for you and Cara."

It was all Matthew could do from hugging the older man in weepy gratitude. The possibility, however remote, of being ejected from managing the boarding-house had been hanging over him like a cloud. Under those circumstances, what would he have to offer a wife? There was the very real possibility that Cara could decide she would be better off returning to Pennsylvania, in which case Matthew would be just as alone as he'd been before. A large part of her reason for answering his ad was his ability to provide for a wife and future family.

"Vielen dank," he murmured to his friend.

Abe nodded. "What I suggest is you look over this space and consider what's necessary to make it a comfortable work environment." The older man explained his vision of the layout and structure of the facility. He concluded, "Keep in mind, Mabel and I are not in a rush to get this done. It will give your parents time to…to adjust to things. Before the point comes where you'd be installing equipment specific to a bakery, you should know whether or not it should become living quarters instead."

Matthew nodded. "I can't express my gratitude for this backup plan, Abe. If we need to use it as an apartment, I'll make it as temporary as I can. But knowing we won't be living in a motel is a relief."

"Well, we wouldn't have let it come to that," replied Abe with a twinkle in his eye. "But it's always *gut* to have alternative arrangements in place. At any rate, it's our hope that this offer will bring you some peace of mind."

"You have no idea how much." Matthew shook Abe's hand. "You and Mabel are gifts from *Gott*."

Abe waved a hand dismissively. "You're a *gut* man, Matthew. And I'm sure Cara is a *gut* woman. We just want to make sure you have the best possible opportunity to start life as a married couple."

Chapter Two

Cara woke up and for a few moments was disoriented. Where was she? Then the events of the previous day flooded over her. She was no longer in Pennsylvania, dealing with her father's anger and her mother's disappointment over Andrew's abandonment. It would have been a thousand times worse had her parents known her fiancé had left her pregnant. Now she was in Montana for a fresh new start. *"Danke, Gott,"* she whispered.

In her letters, she had told Matthew all about Andrew and his abandonment almost at the altar. But she had concealed that she and Andrew had been intimate one time ahead of the wedding. She put a hand on her abdomen. So far she'd had no morning sickness, no illness of any sort. Except for a matter of calendars, she would hardly have known she was pregnant.

She thought about the job ahead, supervising a community cannery. What would happen when the baby was born? A cannery was hard work, and certainly no place for a baby or toddler. Most of the women she'd worked with at her last job in a commercial cannery had been young and unmarried, or older with grown children.

Well, she would trust in *Gott* to provide a solution when the time came.

She dressed carefully, making sure her dress, apron and *kapp* were as neat as she could make them. Then she left her room, quietly descended the stairs and saw Matthew working at the lobby's desk. *"Guder mariye."*

He gave her a broad smile. "*Guder mariye.* How did you sleep?"

"Not bad, considering it's a new place. It's a very nice room."

"I have breakfast for you, if you're hungry."

"Actually I am." Having skipped dinner the night before while pretending to be full—she had been too nervous to eat— she was actually ravenous.

"Can I give you a tour of my private quarters first?"

"*Ja,* sure."

"*Komm* back here, then." He opened a low pass-through gate behind the lobby desk and ushered her into the back.

She stopped on the threshold. "Oh, Matthew, it's lovely."

"*Danke.*" She heard a note of relief in his voice. "It's a bachelor space at the moment, of course, but you're free to change anything at all."

Cara was touched by his eagerness to please. "Show me around."

The area was spacious: an open floor plan for the kitchen and living room, several bedrooms and two bathrooms. He had a wall of books, comfortable furniture and a large braided rag rug that looked homemade. The walls were bare of artwork, in Plain fashion, but were painted a cheerful cream color. There was even a small yard, shaded by a maple tree, with grass, an herb garden and several bird feeders, surrounded by a high and private wall.

"It might not be what you're used to," he apologized, "if you grew up on a farm. But this is a nice town, quiet and welcoming."

"I'm always open to new experiences," she assured him. "Besides, if I'll be canning all day, I may not have time for much else by way of tending a garden or caring for livestock. It's lovely, Matthew. Truly it is."

He smiled, and for a moment she locked eyes with him. He seemed like a kind man. Kindness in a future *hutband* was a big plus in her book. But would that kindness extend to accepting another man's child?

He held her gaze for a heartbeat longer, then looked away. He all but blushed as he moved toward the kitchen. "As I said before, I make an excellent omelet," he offered. "Will that work?"

"*Ja*, sure," she replied. "I'm a decent cook. I have to be, working as a canner. I'm happy to take over meal prep."

"We can split it," he replied easily, cracking eggs into a bowl. He paused for a moment, then looked at her. "I can't tell you how happy I am you're here. I know you're probably nervous—there will be so many new things for you to do and so many people you'll be meeting—but it's my hope you'll find this boardinghouse as an oasis of calm."

Again, she was touched. His words sparked the hint of true affection for this man. "There was a lot of chaos in my own family growing up," she admitted quietly. "My father is a stern man. My brothers and sisters left home as soon as they were able. I'm the youngest, and I think part of why I allowed myself to be courted by Andrew. To be honest, I wasn't all that upset when he left... except, of course, for the humiliation."

"I understand something about the humiliation." He poured the beaten eggs in a pan, then sprinkled chopped green onions and some grated cheese over the top. "The woman I hoped to marry—someone I'd known back in Ohio—decided she didn't want to come to Montana after making all kinds of plans and filling me with hope. She ended up marrying someone else. At least my humiliation happened about two thousand miles away."

"And there was no one here for you to court?"

"Surprisingly, no. We're still a growing church. It's more common for single men to come West than it is for single women.

You might say putting an ad in *The Budget* was an act of desperation." His eyes crinkled with good humor.

"Answering the ad was also an act of desperation," she admitted. "If for no other reason, we should get along well."

"I hope so." He slid the finished omelet onto a plate.

They paused for a silent prayer, then continued chatting while she ate. It occurred to Cara that this could be something she would be doing the rest of her life—talking with Matthew over breakfast. She rather liked the thought.

"Well." He glanced at a clock over the doorway, and rose. "We should probably get going. Yoder's Mercantile opens at nine."

"I'm ready to go." She exhaled, then gave him a smile. "I know I shouldn't be nervous, but I am."

"You'll like the Yoders. They're incredible smart business people, and they're also well-liked by their employees."

Matthew locked the door to his private quarters behind him, but kept the lobby door unlocked. "Have you locked your bedroom door?"

"*Nein.* Should I?"

"It probably would be a *gut* habit to get into. We have two other rooms full at the moment, *Englischers* who are in town visiting relatives, and I always recommend locking your door when other guests are checked in."

"I'll be right back." She dashed up the stairs, locked the door and pocketed the key.

Back downstairs in the lobby, Matthew said to her, "Living in town is different than being on a farm when it comes to security. I'll be sure to make you a duplicate set of building keys for yourself."

"*Danke.*" She looked around her with alert eyes as they emerged from the boardinghouse and walked toward Yoder's Mercantile on the main street.

The store had a broad front porch covered by an awning, with steps in front and a ramp at one end. Pots of colorful mums crowded one side of the porch. The store windows displayed a range of autumn merchandise—crafts, fabrics, soaps, quilts.

Matthew held open the door for her and ushered her inside, where the delicious smells of coffee and baked goods wafted over her.

"Guder mariye!" a woman exclaimed nearby. "You must be Cara."

Cara turned and saw a plump older woman smiling broadly. *"Ja.* Are you Mabel Yoder?" She held out a hand.

Mabel brushed aside the hand and leaned in for a hug instead. "I'm so glad you're here! Everyone has been expecting you. Matthew has been talking of nothing else for days now. Abe! Abraham! Cara is here!"

From a back room, Abe Yoder emerged wearing a canvas work apron over his clothing. *"Welkom, welkom!"* he boomed, and vigorously shook her hand. "So happy you've arrived!"

Cara felt warmth at her new employers' greetings. Matthew had been right about them. She breathed a prayer of gratitude.

"Let me show you around the store," Mabel proposed, "and then I'll show you what we've done so far in the cannery."

"I'll get to work, then." Matthew tipped her a wink and departed.

Mabel walked her through the store and pointed out the bakery section, the coffee shop—where a couple of early customers lingered over laptops—and the selection of dry goods.

"We sell a lot of things made by church members," the older woman explained. "Quilts, soaps, crafts, things like that. We've been wanting to add a selection of home-canned foods as well, but by state law we're not permitted to sell them unless they've been processed in an approved facility. That's one of the many reasons we decided to build our own."

Mabel guided her toward a closed connecting door to the building next door. She opened the door and held it for Cara.

Cara stopped just inside and scanned the echoing facility. Matthew was working on the front portion of the building, installing insulation. He paused and watched her.

Cara took a few steps inside. She was pleased with what she saw. She glanced at Mabel, who was watching her with an anxious look on her face.

"Well?" demanded Mabel. "What do you think?"

"It's *wunderbar*." She walked farther into the large room.

It was a much smaller facility than the one she'd left, but it had everything she needed. There was a commercial steamer to sterilize jars, another steamer designed to slip the skins off tomatoes and peaches, and a large food processor for chopping vegetables. There was a commercial-sized food strainer, numerous propane

burners and four massive pressure canners still in boxes. All the stainless steel
worktables had lockable wheels, and
there were several rolling carts to move
jars and trays of food. Along one wall
was a series of tall rolling carts stacked
with unopened boxes of brand-new canning jars. A high shelf held a series of
kerosene lamps, though adequate lighting came through the building's banks
of high windows along three sides. Some
high stools provided a place to sit while
working at the tables.

She was impressed and gave a low whis-
tle. "This is almost as well equipped as
the huge cannery where I used to work."

Mabel smiled. "We did a lot of research to learn what kind of equipment
we should get."

"I have books and notebooks with recipes for some of the specialties we sold
in Pennsylvania. Once I obtain the ingredients, I can start canning some of them
right away for sale in the store."

"*Ja gut!* That's what we were hoping. But a lot of women in the church might be hoping to use the facility to can their garden produce, or have you do it for them."

"And how many of them want to water-bath their carrots?" Cara asked with a twinge of humor. Water-bath processing of vegetables was a common and dangerous mistake.

"More than you'd think," admitted Mabel. "It's another reason we won't sell home-canned goods in the store, except for the occasional jar of jam. We can't be sure they're safe."

"Well, that's one promise I can give you. Anything coming out of this facility will be processed properly. It's one of the reasons I'm so passionate about canning—I think it's an incredible method to preserve food, but only if done the correct way."

Mabel flashed her a grin. "I think we're going to get along very well, Cara. *Welkom* aboard."

* * *

Matthew busied himself with assessing the other half of the building and taking measurements, which he wrote down on a clipboard. He was able to listen to Cara and Mabel's conversation about the cannery. He was impressed. Cara knew her stuff when it came to food preservation. She was confident and clearly experienced.

"...so if I can order up some of the ingredients I need, I can begin producing some things you can sell in the store right away," he heard her say.

"*Ja*, make a list," agreed Mabel. "But I think you'll find many of the ingredients you'll need can be found locally. We have a man in our church who runs a B and B nearby. He prides himself on providing meals for his guests with nothing but local foods."

"*Gut!*" Matthew saw Cara's eyes shine. "That means I can get started all the sooner. One of the commercial recipes I brought with me is a peach salsa. It's out of this world."

Mabel chuckled. "If you like, I'll go through your recipes with you and select the ones we'd like to carry in the store."

"Ja gut," replied Cara. "Let me go back to the boardinghouse and get my reference books."

"That's fine. I'll be in the store."

The older woman went through the connecting door into the retail space, and Cara walked up to Matthew. "I'm going to dash back to my room and get my reference books," she told him. "You said the boardinghouse front door is unlocked?"

"Ja, but you'll need your room key."

"In my pocket." She patted her apron.

"Would you like company on the walk?"

She eyed him with what seemed like amusement. "Can you leave your job?"

"Ja, sure. I simply work the hours I need

to. I'm not a full-time contractor for the Yoders."

"Then *ja*, I'd like the company."

Matthew snatched up his straw hat and plopped it on his head. "Let's go through the store so I can let Abe know I'm going with you."

In a few minutes, they were out in the warm September sunshine. "What do you think of the job and cannery so far?" he asked her.

"It's lovely." She hugged herself and smiled that incredible smile at him. "It's such a beautiful little facility. I can't believe they're putting me in charge of it. I think I'm going to be very happy here, Matthew."

"For sure and certain I hope so." His heart swelled with gratitude to *Gott* for sending him a woman with such enthusiasm.

An idea occurred to him. "There's a walking path along a creek on the edge of town," he suggested. "Would you like to go for a walk this afternoon after work is finished? It might be a nice way to blow the cobwebs from our brains."

"*Ja*, sure." She gave him a shy smile. "We need to get this courtship started, don't we?"

"I agree," he said in relief. There was so much he wanted to know about her. What were her interests besides food preservation? What was her favorite color? Could she hold a tune while singing? How many brothers and sisters did she have? Maybe he should make a list...

It was a strange thing, courting a stranger. It seems they were both single for similar reasons—the ones they planned to marry had married someone else—but beyond that, she was a mystery to him. And he couldn't wait to solve that mystery.

He held open the door to the boarding-house lobby for her. "I'll only be a moment," she said, heading up the stairs and disappearing from view.

Sure enough, she reappeared within five minutes, her arms laden with books and a large notebook. "Here, I can carry them," he offered.

"*Danke.* We can split the load."

He took the heaviest of the volumes and they headed back to the mercantile. "Will you keep these in the cannery?"

"*Ja.* They're not just my collection of recipes. They're also the reference books I'll need to make sure I'm processing everything according to health guidelines."

"How did you fall into this line of work, anyway?"

"My grandmother first taught me to can when I was five or six years old," she replied. "*Grossmammi* was something of a lifeline for me since my parents weren't...weren't always easy to live with. She taught me to lift myself above my difficult home life. I owe her a lot." She looked grave.

"She's gone?" he inquired as tactfully as he could.

"Ja." She blinked hard. "I think losing her is what made me accept courtship from someone like Andrew. I—I guess I was lonely, and without *Grossmammi* there wasn't really anyone else I could turn to."

He tried to keep his tone light. "I wonder what your *grossmammi* would have to say about becoming a mail-order bride?"

To his surprise, a snort of laughter escaped her. "She'd probably think it was funny. *Grossmammi* had quite a sense of humor. Also, I think she would approve of leaving my parents behind. I think it bothered her that her own daughter, my *mamm*, turned into such a frightened individual as a result of my father's dominance. That's not how my *grossdaddi* was, and she never really cared for my *daed*."

He spoke carefully. "That's why I want you to be certain you'll be happy before we get married. I have no problem courting a whole year and getting married next

November, just to be certain. I don't want you to feel trapped as your mother must feel."

She was silent a moment, walking beside him with her armful of books. "That's kind of you, Matthew," she said in a somewhat strangled voice. "But I feel certain I'll be ready to get married in November. I—I just hope you will be too."

"Why wouldn't I be?"

She shrugged as they climbed the porch steps to the mercantile. "Maybe I'm just cynical after Andrew's desertion, but I believe sometimes people aren't what they seem."

There was no more time for conversation as she went off to collaborate with Mabel. Matthew had no more excuses to linger, so he deposited the books on the store's front counter and retreated to the other building, where he resumed his carpentry work.

But it was as if a warning bell had sounded in his head. Why wouldn't he be ready to get married in November? He was the one who had advertised for a bride, ain't so? He was *more* than ready to get married.

In light of her disastrous romantic past, she had a right to be wary, but she was correct in one regard: sometimes people weren't what they seemed.

He needed to look beyond her beauty and smile to understand the complex woman underneath. After all, there was no room for error. Once they were married, they would be married for life. He didn't want to make a mistake, as her own parents had. For this reason, he was pleased she was open to courting.

Several hours later, strolling beside Cara on a gravel path beside a small creek, he jokingly ran through the list of questions he'd thought of earlier.

"Green," she said promptly. "It's been my favorite color for as long as I can remember. I've always loved earth tones—

greens and browns and dark reds and such."

He chuckled. "I prefer brown myself, and I like green too. I have four siblings, by the way. How about you?"

"There are six of us. I have three brothers, two sisters. I'm the youngest. My older brothers and sisters are all married, and they married fairly young. I think everyone was eager to leave home."

"Are their marriages happy?"

"*Ja*, so far as I know."

"Can you sing?" he asked her.

"What is this, an interview?" Her eyes crinkled with amusement. "I *can* sing. Whether or not I sing *well* is anyone's guess. I can keep a tune and won't embarrass myself in church."

"*Ja*, it's something of an interview. There's just so much about you I'm eager to know. For example, what are your interests besides canning?"

"Hmm. Reading. Jigsaw puzzles on snowy nights. I like writing, too—I've had a few pieces appear in *The Budget* on the subject of canning. I've thought about writing a book about food preservation."

"What a *wunderbar* idea! I know Mabel and Abe would carry such a book in their store."

"Turnaround is fair play," said Cara. They came to the end of the gravel walkway where it dead-ended against a farmer's field, and turned around to walk back to town. "What are your interests besides carpentry and running a boardinghouse? And can you sing?"

He chuckled. "I'm not too bad a singer. As for interests, I like fishing. I also like taking nature walks, like we're doing now. It's probably because I live in town and don't see as much wildlife as I wish. I do a bit of bird-watching, and in winter fill the bird feeders in the backyard. I see my parents or sister or brother fairly often. Two of my siblings remained back in Ohio, but I have a brother and sister here in Montana. I think you'll like them.

And of course, I'm dragged into every work party that takes place on the settlement. We still have people moving here from back East, so we often have work parties to build a home or barn or some other structure."

"Well, it's better than my ex-fiancé," she said tartly. "Andrew didn't have a lot going for him besides carpentry."

Matthew wondered what she had seen in this Andrew fellow that made her think he would be a suitable life partner before his desertion. He chalked up her attitude to the natural bitterness she must feel. He'd felt similar bitterness after the woman he had been courting back in Ohio broke it off. It had left him feeling much more lonely than he expected.

Shifting his mind back to the present, he said, "I know you answered my ad in *The Budget* because you were anxious to get away from everything back in Pennsylvania," he remarked. "But whatever the circumstances, I'm glad you're here."

The knee-weakening smile she flashed him seemed tinged with strain. "*Danke*, Matthew. I hope you never regret deciding to take a chance with me."

Matthew was surprised by her comment. She was everything he'd asked *Gott* to send him in a wife. What kind of regrets could he possibly have?

Chapter Three

It was such a pleasure for Matthew to work in the same space as Cara. He delighted in being near her. While he began the process of finishing the new bakery, his future wife spent her first full day in the cannery thoroughly exploring her new workspace. She peered into cabinets, poked under tables and opened drawers. She unboxed the pristine pressure canners and smiled at the contents.

"What do you think?" he asked, snapping open a tape measure and marking a spot on a batt of insulation.

"It's *wunderschön*," she replied. She

gifted him with the full force of her smile. "I don't think the Yoders spared any expense. Everything is top-notch and brand-new." She chuckled. "I almost hate to dirty anything up."

"Well, that strikes me as your job, so I wouldn't hesitate." He grinned at her enthusiasm. "You're like a kid in a candy store. What *is* all this equipment, anyway?"

She launched into an explanation of all the equipment, leaving Matthew relieved he wasn't the one who had to operate any of it.

"Whew." Matthew whistled when she finished the tour. "I'm glad you know your way around this. I'd be lost."

"I've been working my way around the commercial-grade equipment for three years now. I know it like the back of my hand." She glanced around the cannery, and he saw a satisfied smile on her face.

"My mother and sisters can food," observed Matthew, "but I know they only do so because they *have* to, not necessarily because they *want* to. I have a feeling you'll have no shortage of work. And," he added, "I suspect I'll be building a pantry in the boardinghouse. I think you'll need the space, *ja*?"

Her brown eyes twinkled at him in a way that brought butterflies to his stomach. "You know how they say the best way to a man's heart is through his stomach? Well, the best way to my heart is to give me pantry space. Enough shelves, and I'm all yours."

"I'll keep that in mind," he croaked, then cleared his throat. "In fact, you can design your pantry however you like, and I'll make it to order."

"*Danke*, Matthew." The moment of sheer flirtation between them boded well for the future. She seemed happy and confident, pleased with her work situation—and, apparently, warming up to him as well.

He wanted to fall in love with her, *ja*. But he also wanted to fall in *like* with her.

On the surface, she was everything he could hope for in a wife. He knew looks could be deceiving, and he also knew he was firmly in the heady, initial stages of infatuation, but what could go wrong? She seemed so right for him.

Lost in his thoughts, he didn't hear her cross the room as she came to his side. "Now tell me what you're building here," she invited.

He tamped down his reaction to her nearness and focused on her question, making sure not to confess Abe's plan to use the space as a temporary apartment if necessary. "Abe and Mabel are considering opening an in-house bakery," he explained. "As you can see, there's a lot of work to be done before it can be used for anything. I was too busy getting the cannery finished before your arrival to give this space much thought, but now I'll be installing insulation, walls, flooring, that kind of thing. Oh, and a woodstove. Abe wanted that put in sooner rather than later, since the weather will be getting chilly soon."

"A bakery is a *gut* idea! The cannery where I used to work was in a touristy village. It had an Amish bakery that was very popular."

A thought suddenly occurred to Matthew. "Will you ever be teaching any canning classes? If so, I can probably shoehorn in some classroom space."

"For sure and certain. But any classes will be in the kitchen area, not in a classroom setting. People need hands-on experience." She tilted her head a bit. "Have the Yoders hired a baker?"

"*Nein.* It's far too soon to think about it. But Abe mentioned they might add another connecting door into the store there…" he pointed "…or even remove a section of wall for a bakery display area."

"Is the town big enough to support these businesses economically?"

"So far, *ja*. Pierce is the county seat, so it serves a lot of smaller outlying towns. The town may seem remote—and it is—but there are five or six even smaller communities in the area. This county is huge, almost the size of New Jersey, but only has about sixteen thousand people in the entire county."

"Wow." Her eyebrows rose. "Those are some impressive statistics."

"*Ja*. And the townspeople have been very welcoming to us. Did you know there wasn't even a café before the Yoders opened their store? Their coffee area has become quite popular among the *Englisch*. Since I live so close, Abe Yoder keeps me busy whenever a new project crops up. I work at my own convenience when I'm not busy at the boardinghouse."

"Matthew..." Cara paused and bit her lip. "I know you said finances weren't a problem, but are you truly able to support a family? When babies come, my work at the cannery will be limited, though I can still act in a supervisory role."

"Ja," he said. "I wouldn't have advertised for a wife if I wasn't in a financial position to support a family. Of that you can be assured." Normally the financial prospect of courting couples was no secret, but they were still strangers to each other. She deserved to know everything—though he wasn't yet ready to confess his parents' stubborn opposition to advertising for a bride, or how it might impact his future financial security.

"Gut." She smiled. "I'm grateful to you, Matthew. You allowed me to escape what was becoming an intolerable situation in Pennsylvania, and landed me among what seem to be very nice people. *Gott ist gut."*

Matthew couldn't agree more. Hopefully, his parents would agree.

He knew he was taking a chance on requesting a mail-order bride, but it seemed

Gott had answered his prayers as much as hers. He only hoped he could live up to her expectations on what she wanted in a *hutband*.

But even if he missed the mark somehow, he knew married couples often grew and changed together. Just look at his parents. Just look at his sister and brother-in-law. Just look at the Yoders. In each case—especially among the older couples—even the ones who hadn't known each other long had grown extremely fond of each other.

He would become the kind of *hutband* Cara wanted. He would strive to incorporate the biblical advice of love. He would be kind. He would not be envious. He wouldn't boast or be proud. He wouldn't be easily angered. He would keep no record of wrongs. He would protect, trust and persevere.

In short, he was determined to do everything in his power to make Cara happy.

* * *

Cara's first few days at the cannery were satisfying ones. With the Yoders' help, she was able to pull together all the ingredients she needed for her first canning project, peach salsa. It was Matthew's inspiration to put a prominent sign both in the store's window as well as at the cash register, announcing Today's Specialty: Fresh Peach Salsa! Mabel suggested having one jar available for taste tests. On that first day, she produced thirty quarts of peach salsa and the Yoders sold every last one of them.

Mabel and Abe were delighted at the fast success. Already they were planning on rearranging portions of the store to accommodate Cara's selection of canned goods.

Thomas Kemp, the store's bookkeeper, told her, "My sister wants to meet you. She just had a baby at the same time everything in the garden is ripening. She was hoping you could do some of the canning for her."

"*Ja*, sure!" exclaimed Cara. "That's what I'm here for. The Yoders want this to be available to the public for a small fee, as long as I supervise the process. For anything not being sold in the store, I'm asking people to supply their own jars and lids, but I can handle the rest."

"I have a lady offering to sell me some of her homegrown blueberries," chimed in Mabel. "She said she can part with about a hundred pounds of frozen fruit. Can you use it?"

"Of course!" Cara grinned. "I can make blueberry jam or blueberry-peach butter or blueberry pie filling. Which would you prefer?"

"All of the above?" Mabel suggested, chuckling. "I have a feeling we'll be hiring an assistant for you very soon. If things go as planned, having someone to help chop and peel will be a big help."

"*Ja*, it would." Cara intended to make

sure they hired that assistant. While no one knew of her pregnancy yet, canning was a physically demanding job. Having an assistant would help tremendously. "Do you have someone in mind?"

"*Nein*, not at the moment," admitted Mabel. "Perhaps a *youngie*, or maybe an older woman?"

"Either would work. If it's a *youngie*, I can train her in correct canning procedures. If it's an older woman, she'll bring experience with her."

"I'll keep an eye out for someone in the community I think might be suitable." Mabel went over to the store to start closing down for the night.

Cara finished her day by cleaning the canning area, making sure it was sanitized for tomorrow's activities. Then, if he wasn't already in the building, Matthew made it a habit to walk over to the mercantile to escort her back to the boardinghouse for the evening, a gentlemanly gesture Cara found charming.

"I thought about getting started on building you that pantry," her future *hutband* remarked on the walk. "You can let me know how you'd like it built."

Cara grinned. "Should I consider this something like a wedding present?"

"Perhaps." He locked eyes with her for a few seconds. Cara felt herself blush. "One of the advantages of living in the boardinghouse is it has so much room. You can make the pantry as big as you wish."

"Be careful what you say," she joked. "I definitely have some plans in my head for what would make a suitable pantry."

"Whatever plans you envision, I can make it a reality," he assured her.

Cara knew he was referring to a carpentry project, but for a moment his words took on a deeper meaning. Her plans for a family life—could he make that a reality? The unborn child growing within her—could he accept it as his own? She had to resist the urge to cradle her still-flat midsection protectively. She had a limited amount of time to get to know Matthew before she would be forced to admit her condition.

Matthew was a man of his word. After dinner, he picked up a tape measure and a clipboard with paper. "Now let's discuss the pantry. What should it look like?"

"Let me sketch out my thoughts." Cara took the clipboard and pencil from him, then started sketching. "Ideally it would be a room with shelves lining three sides, plus as much of the fourth side that isn't a doorway. Then in the center..." she sketched some more "...a set of stand-alone shelves accessible from all sides. Walkways would be about thirty inches wide, shelves about twelve inches deep." She showed him the sketch. "What do you think?"

He laughed out loud. "I think you know exactly what you want. How long have you been thinking this through?"

She caught the humor. "A long time," she

admitted. "Some little girls dream about this or that. Me, I've always dreamed about my ideal pantry. Is this design possible?"

"You're talking to a carpenter trying to please his future wife," declared Matthew. "Of course it's possible."

In that moment, Cara knew she could easily fall in love with him. Not just because he was willing to build her the pantry of her dreams, but because he was so transparently ready to become a family man. She felt like hugging him, but knew it was too much too soon.

"What's wrong?" He was watching her.

"I—I'm a little overwhelmed," she admitted. "No one has ever been as kind and generous to me as you have. I don't know if I deserve it," she added in a grimmer tone than she anticipated.

"Did your father never show such kindness to your mother?"

"Not really. He was never abusive, you understand, just…rigid. I know my

mother would have loved a large pantry,
for example, but I don't think she ever
dared to ask. That's the example of mat-
rimony I saw growing up."

"But it wasn't *my* example," he told her.
"My mother will happily show you the
pantry *Daed* built her. My parents are *gut*
people, and that's the example I'll bring
into our marriage." His voice quivered for
a moment. "By the way, my parents have
been away on a trip visiting relatives back
in Ohio, but they're home now. They've
invited us for dinner tomorrow."

"Your parents." In the activities of
the last few days, she'd forgotten about
his family. It added a whole new level
of complexity to her situation. While
she was sure she could charm his parents upon meeting them, how would they
feel about their son marrying a pregnant
woman? "How did your *mamm* and *daed*
feel about you putting an ad in *The Budget* for a wife?" she asked.

"They weren't too happy," he admitted.

He placed the clipboard on the kitchen table and started making tea. "But I'm hoping they'll come around."

"I hope they'll like me…"

"Nervous?"

"*Ja*, of course. Wouldn't you be?"

"I suppose." He poured hot water over the English Breakfast tea he knew she liked by now. "But I'm sure my parents will like you. And at some point you'll meet my brother Mark, and my sister Eva Hostetler and her family."

The sheer affection in his voice for his family members created some envy in Cara. While she loved her brothers and sisters, she had a more complicated relationship with her own parents. She realized how much she coveted the good opinion of his family, which, *Gott* willing, would become her own family in a short period of time.

Unless, of course, Matthew rejected her because of her condition. If that happened—and it wasn't too unlikely—then she would not only lose her prospective *hutband*, but the loving family he brought with him. It was an enormous price to pay for the mistake she made with Andrew.

But all that was in the future. She still had some time to figure out the details of how to convince Matthew she was worth marrying.

Chapter Four

The next morning, Cara was busy preparing a batch of the promised blueberry pie filling when Thomas Kemp, the store's bookkeeper, walked into the cannery, carrying a large box of vegetables. He was chatting with a pretty woman about Cara's age who was carrying an infant in her arms.

Thomas placed the box on the counter. "Cara, I'd like you to meet my sister, Miriam Lapp. Miriam, this is Cara Lengacher. I'll just go get the rest of the produce," he added to his sister. He grabbed the wheeled cart kept under the counter and disappeared through the connecting doorway into the store.

"Guten tag," greeted Cara. She wiped her hands on a towel and reached over to shake Miriam's hand. "Thomas mentioned you wanted me to can your garden's harvest because of the new *boppli.*"

"Ja." Miriam smiled as she shook Cara's hand. "This little fellow only arrived three weeks ago, and instead of trying to do everything, I thought it would be easier to hand the canning over to you."

"Of course." Cara was envious at the bundle in Miriam's arms. Soon enough, she would be holding her own bundle. "What's your *sohn's* name?"

"Isaac." Miriam angled her body so the sleeping infant's face was more visible. "It's the first time I've been on the birthing end of babies, so to speak. Usually I'm the one delivering them."

"Oh, are you a midwife?"

"Ja."

Cara knew she would be needing her services shortly. "May I hold him?"

"Of course." Miriam transferred the bundle into Cara's arms.

Cara had held newborns numerous times over the years, and never failed to enjoy the experience. But now, the reality of her own condition made her pay attention to the weight and feel of the child in her arms. Little Isaac was sound asleep, his rosebud lips making tiny smacking movements.

"He's beautiful," she breathed. "And such a handsome little man."

"Danke." Miriam's face softened. "My *hutband*, Aaron, thinks so too. You'll meet him soon enough," she added. "He just slipped out to do some errands in town. I should warn you in advance, his face is heavily scarred from a fire several years ago. I would ask you not to react too strongly when you first see him. It's taken him some time to climb out of his shell."

"Of course." Considering how pretty

Miriam was, Cara suspected the bond between her and her *hutband* was strong indeed to overcome a disfiguring accident.

"Aaron thinks Isaac looks like him," continued Miriam. "He tells me he used to be a handsome man before the fire, and now Isaac will continue that legacy."

"That's sweet." Cara handed the infant back to his mother. "I'll bet he's such a proud father."

"Oh, he is." Miriam's face took on a glow of love. "I'm the most blessed of women."

Seeing the transparent love Miriam felt for her husband, Cara almost had to blink back tears. She hoped she would find that same love with Matthew one day.

"Tell me what you have for me to can up," she said, turning to the box of vegetables. "I see carrots, corn…"

Miriam nodded as Thomas returned, with several more boxes on the cart. "Typical September harvest."

Thomas heaved the boxes of vegetables

on the counter. "Another load of vegetables, and then I'll get the jars," he told his sister. He wheeled the cart out to the buggy again.

"Do you want them canned up in any specific recipe, such as chutneys or mixed vegetables?" inquired Cara, peering into the various boxes. "Or do you want just straight jars of the various vegetables?"

"Straight jars. That way I can combine the vegetables any way I like." Miriam shifted her son's position so the baby rested over her shoulder. "Also, I don't want to make this any harder on you."

Cara chuckled. "*Nein*, canning is fun," she replied. "To me, there's something satisfying about taking raw vegetables and turning them into something that will last a long time on a pantry shelf. And with all this new equipment, it's a lot easier than you might think to get the job done. The Yoders said they would charge a small fee for each finished jar, as long as you provide the jars and lids. Is that all right?"

"Of course. I expected it."

Cara reached over and took a clipboard and pen. "Now tell me what size jars you want."

She wrote down specifics—green beans in pints, corn in quarts, tomatoes turned into both sauce and paste, then canned in pints—as Thomas trundled back and forth, bringing in more boxes.

"Ten boxes. That's all," he announced at last, parking the wheeled cart in its slot under the counter.

"*Danke*, Thomas." Miriam smiled at her brother, who returned her smile and slipped out of the cannery to return to work in the mercantile.

"He's a nice fellow," commented Cara, peering into the various boxes and mentally assessing the task ahead.

"*Ja*, he is." Miriam looked thoughtful. "He went through a rough patch, but with *Gott's* help he completely turned his life around and is one of the best men I know. Speaking of which, where's Matthew?" she added, glancing over at the unfinished construction area at the front of the building.

"He went to fetch some items from the hardware store."

Miriam nodded. "What do you think of him?" she asked in a conspiratorial tone.

"You mean for my *hutband*?"

"*Ja.* Sending away for a mail-order bride is not the normal way things are done in our community. The whole church has been wondering how you two would get along now that you've met."

Cara paused and turned to her new friend. "I think he's *wunnerschee*," she said softly. "I was nervous to meet him, as you can imagine, but he seems like such a *gut* man that I thank *Gott* for him."

"*Macht's gut*, then." Miriam looked pleased. "I know it was a chance both of you took."

"*Ja.* Matthew has offered that we wait

until next November to get married, but
I—I think I would be fine marrying this
coming November."

"Are you sure? Waiting another year
won't make a difference if you'll be
joined for a lifetime."

Waiting another year would make an
enormous difference—for Cara. When
he learned the truth of her situation, who
knew whether Matthew would still want
to marry her? But she could hardly tell
this to Miriam on such short acquaintance. Besides, no one knew she was
pregnant, not even her own parents.

At the pause in the conversation, Miriam looked at her sharply. "Cara?"

"Sorry." Cara wiped a hand over her
face and smiled at Miriam, hoping to dis-
pel any suspicions. "Just thinking."

"Matthew is well-regarded in our
church," Miriam said. "Everyone thinks
highly of him. We knew it was difficult
for him to remain unmarried simply because there weren't any eligible women in

the community, so you can imagine how eager everyone is to meet you."

"I—I hope I can live up to everyone's expectations," Cara stuttered. She knew she would have to work hard to garner good faith ahead of the big reveal. "It's a little nerve-wracking."

"*Ja*, but we have a nice group of people out here. I don't think you'll have any problems settling in."

"I'll be meeting his parents tonight," said Cara, beginning to remove vegetables from the cartons and stacking them in piles. "They've invited us to dinner. I'm trying not to be nervous about it. Mabel said I can bring them a couple jars of the blueberry pie filling I'm canning up today as a gift."

"Matthew's parents are lovely people," assured Miriam. "I'm sure they'll like you very much."

"I hope you're right. I have a strained relationship with my own parents," she confessed, "so I'm eager to look on Matthew's family as mine too."

"Eli and Anna are salt of the earth," assured Miriam. "They have generous hearts, and I'm sure they're excited to welcome you as their newest daughter."

"Matthew said they weren't too happy with how he went about finding a wife. I'll have to work to win them over, I'm sure." Cara sighed. "And then, of course, I'll meet the rest of the community on Sunday. In a way, I'll be glad when all the introductions are over. I can't help but feel I'm under a microscope."

"By next week, it should all be easier, since everyone will have met you. Would you and Matthew like to come to dinner sometime at our farm?" she added. "I know Aaron and Matthew get along well, and I'd like to get to know you better too."

"*Danke*, I'd like that!" Cara smiled at Miriam.

Before she could say anything more,

Matthew walked into the cannery, carrying some bags from the hardware store. Cara considered it a good sign that her insides gave a little jump at his return.

He smiled at Miriam. "*Guten tag.* How's the *boppli*?"

"Hale and healthy." Miriam patted her son's back. "I was just getting acquainted with your bride."

"She's invited us to their house for dinner sometime," said Cara.

"*Ja gut,*" replied Matthew. "Let us know the day, and we'll be there. I just saw Aaron in the hardware store," he added. "He'll be along shortly."

Miriam nodded. "I'll introduce him to Cara, then we'll be off."

"I should have all the canning done for you by the middle of next week," said Cara.

"It's a big relief to hand the project over to you," admitted Miriam. "The timing of this little one's birth couldn't have been worse as far as preserving the garden. I'll talk to Mabel about what she'll charge me for your services."

At that moment, a man with a heavily scarred face walked into the cannery through the connecting door. Because of Miriam's warning, Cara made sure to keep her expression pleasant as she was introduced.

Aaron Lapp might have scars, but she saw he had, indeed, once been a handsome man…especially when he looked at his wife. His eyes held such an expression of love that Cara felt her emotions rise.

Would she and Matthew ever have such a relationship?

In the late afternoon after work, Matthew and Cara headed back toward the boardinghouse, each of them cradling jars of blueberry pie filling in their arms. "Nervous?" he asked.

"Ja." Cara kept her eyes on the ground. "I just hope your parents like me."

"Cara…" Matthew hesitated. "I haven't

wanted to worry you, but it's important you make a *gut* impression tonight. My parents weren't happy with the mail-order bride situation, and…well, I should let you know they own the boardinghouse, not me."

She stopped on the sidewalk, staring at him with concern. "You mean, if they don't like me, there's a possibility you might lose your job?"

"Well…*ja*."

He braced himself for her anger. Frankly he wouldn't blame her. If the worst happened and his parents disowned him, he had nothing he could offer a wife except his sporadic carpentry work and Abe Yoder's humble promise of a temporary place to live.

With the stakes so high, he was relieved when Cara simply smiled and said, "Then I'll do my best to make a *gut* impression."

In that moment, Matthew knew he had chosen well. Cara was obviously a woman of rare strength and courage.

Back in the boardinghouse, he put the jars of pie filling on the check-in desk. "If you want to freshen up, I'll go hitch up the horse," he offered. "I'll find a box for the jars as well."

"Danke." She placed her jars on the desk and disappeared upstairs.

It only took a few minutes to hitch the horse to the close-fronted buggy. Lubelle was a standardbred horse he'd owned for years. She was a docile, sturdy animal with a shiny brown coat. He snatched up a cardboard box from the stables and brought it back into the house. Cara was already waiting for him. She had changed into a dark green dress and white apron, and looked becoming.

"Ready?" he asked unnecessarily.

"Ja," she replied. "Let's go convince your parents that I'm a *gut* catch."

He chuckled, trying to control his own nervousness. His parents were fine people and he doubted they would say or do anything inappropriate, but tonight's dinner could conceivably set in motion a series of events he didn't want.

But he didn't say anything as he assisted her into the buggy, climbed into his own seat, took up the reins and clucked to the horse.

"Will there be anyone else at dinner besides your parents?" Cara inquired. She sat demurely, her hands in her lap, as the horse trotted out of town toward the Amish settlement.

"I don't think my brother or sister are going to be at dinner tonight," he replied. "I think my parents wanted to meet you first without too many other people around."

"What are your parents like?" she asked him.

"They're *gut* people." He spoke honestly. "I love them, of course, but more than that, I like them. That's why their hostility toward my methods of finding a wife is so disturbing. Not," he added with some sarcasm, "that they've offered much by way of feasible alternatives. There simply aren't any available single women out here. And I want a family."

She touched him lightly on the arm. "I promise not to do or say anything that might make them dislike me."

Matthew felt better as the horse made its way toward his parents' farm.

"That's their farm." He pointed toward an older white clapboard house with a large newish barn nearby. "My *daed* refuses to give up his cows," he added with a smile, "which is why they're not the ones running the boardinghouse, even though they bought it."

"And you're happy running it?" she asked, "rather than farming?"

"*Ja*. Maybe someday, after *Daed* wants to retire, I might take over the farm, but for the moment I like working at the boardinghouse."

He guided the horse up the drive and pulled to a halt by the hitching post near the front of the house. In moments his parents, Eli and Anna, had emerged onto the porch. They smiled, but knowing them as he did, Matthew saw strain and concern they were trying to disguise.

He could almost feel Cara tense up beside him. He felt pretty tense himself. He waved to them in greeting, as Eli Miller descended the stairs.

"Let me help you down, my dear," the older man said politely, as he held out a hand to Cara.

She smiled, took his hand and stepped out of the buggy. *"Danke."*

Anna Miller, Matthew's mother, approached. "It's nice to meet you, Cara." She held out her hand with an overtone of stiffness, though her smile was polite enough.

Watching his future wife's face, Matthew knew she couldn't guess that his parents were seldom this tight-laced. Most of the time they were warm and friendly. But at least they were polite. Matthew thanked *Gott* for that.

"How was your trip West?" inquired his *mamm* as she led Cara into the house.

"It was fine. Long," replied Cara. Matthew noticed how she kept her smile in place and gave every indication of being relaxed and at ease, though he knew she wasn't. "Matthew put me in the prettiest room in the boardinghouse. It's such a beautiful building."

Matthew followed, carrying the box of blueberry pie filling while watching Cara. He tried to interpret her body language for clues on how she felt about his parents. After all, if everything went as planned, they would become her parents too.

On the surface, everything seemed fine. His mother gave Cara a small task in the kitchen to set her at ease as she bustled around setting the table for dinner.

"She's lovely, *sohn*," his *daed* quietly said to him. There was a certain amount of surprise in his voice.

Matthew turned to his father. "I think

so too," he replied guardedly. "*Gott* has certainly answered my prayers."

"I hope she's everything she seems."

He felt a wave of annoyance. "I have no reason to doubt it. She's been here a week and dived right into work at the cannery. The Yoders think the world of her."

"That's *gut*," his *daed* admitted. Matthew knew his father admired the Yoders' judgment in business matters. "It's necessary to have more than just a pretty face in a wife. I hope that's the case with Cara."

"From everything I've seen so far, she has a sweet disposition to match. Don't pick at her, *Daed*. She's nervous enough as it is, meeting you and *Mamm*."

To his relief, his *daed* smiled and clapped him on the back. "I won't, I promise. Now let's go see how she's doing with your *mamm*."

As the evening progressed, Matthew felt cautiously optimistic. His *mamm* drew Cara into discussions about canning, and expressed gratitude for the blueberry pie filling. "One of Eli's favorite desserts," she said. "How are you getting on with the Yoders?"

"Very well," replied Cara. "They're smart, those people! The whole facility is sparkling new and of the highest standards. Mabel said she is willing to hire an assistant for me, especially as things get busier. I think I'm going to be very happy there. Do you need me to can any of your garden harvest?" she added.

Matthew's *mamm* chuckled. "Believe it or not, child, I enjoy canning almost as much as you do. Eli plants such a large garden every year that I have my hands full, but I'm always glad for the surplus."

"Matthew said you have a lovely pantry," offered Cara.

"*Ja*, my Eli, he built it for me." Anna smiled. "Would you like to see it?"

"For sure and certain!"

Without apology, Anna abandoned the men at the table, taking Cara with her to show off her favorite room in the house. Matthew noted his father's bemused expression at being so unceremoniously deserted.

"What is it about women and pantries?" he inquired, spooning up the last of his mother's chicken casserole. He could hear exclamations and animated conversation coming from the enclosed food storage room.

"I've always said your mother is the quartermaster of the home," *Daed* remarked. "That's why it's important to have a place to put things. Cara probably feels the same way."

"I've offered to build a pantry in the boardinghouse according to her design," admitted Matthew.

Daed nodded. "I won't say I'm completely enamored with how you went about finding a wife, but hopefully she'll work out for you, *sohn*."

Matthew wondered why his parents were so opposed to him advertising for a wife in *The Budget*. It was not like he would be forced to marry Cara. If they were incompatible, they would simply part ways, no one worse for the wear. There was a story here, something he didn't know. He intended to find out one day...

Just then, Cara and his mother emerged from the pantry. "You should see it!" exclaimed Cara, her eyes glowing. "It's perfect! That flour sifter—what a wonderful idea."

"I've seen it," Matthew assured her. "In fact, I helped build it. And if you like the flour sifter, I can make one for your pantry as well."

"*Danke*, Matthew!" She smiled that beautiful smile at him. "I may take you up on that."

After dinner, dessert and visiting, Matthew assisted Cara back into the buggy and watched as she waved enthusiastically to his parents, who stood on the front porch to see them off.

"What do you think of them?" he asked once they were out of earshot.

She sighed with what sounded like relief. "They seemed to like me. For my part, I liked them very much, your *mamm* especially."

"You and *Mamm* certainly had a lot to talk about," he said with a laugh.

"Her pantry! It's *wunnerschee*. Though I expect," she added impishly, "that mine will be even better when you're finished with it."

"Especially if it has a flour sifter," he teased, then turned serious. "I know *Daed* seemed... I don't know, maybe *reassured* is the right word, at meeting you."

She sighed. "I know this is probably rough on you," she said. "I do hope your parents can look upon me as a daughter after we get married."

"At least the evening went well." He covered her hand with his, and was gratified when she laced her fingers with his.

At her silence, he glanced at her. She

had a somber look on her face. After a moment, she said, "I hope I'll always be worthy of your parents' acceptance."

Matthew was puzzled by her comment. He had just witnessed what he hoped would be a growing friendship between his parents and his future wife. What could possibly be clouding Cara's feelings on the matter? "What do you mean?"

"Nothing." She looked out at the dusky landscape. "Sometimes I have a tendency to question Providence, that's all. Pay me no heed, Matthew."

Her comment didn't worry him over-much, but it *did* remind him that he had, after all, only just met the woman. There was still a lot he had to learn about her.

Chapter Five

Matthew clucked to the horse and started the buggy toward the outskirts of town. "Another first for you."

Cara glanced at him, sitting beside her on the buggy seat as he guided the horse deeper into the valley where the Amish settlement was located. "You mean attending my first church service here in Montana? *Ja*, but I'm not nearly as nervous about it as I was at meeting your parents."

"I suspect they've been talking about you ever since."

She forced a smile. She felt the beginnings of affection for his parents, along with just the tiniest annoyance that they held the financial purse strings over Matthew. Yet part of her desperately wanted to look upon them as her own parents. How would they feel when they learned Matthew's prospective bride was already pregnant?

"Tell me about the settlement." She gestured toward the broad valley punctuated by stretches of conifers and wide fields dotted with cattle or cultivated with crops.

"It was once a huge ranch," he told her. "A couple thousand acres or something. When it went up for sale, no one was interested in buying it because it was so big. The church was able to purchase it for a decent price, and has been portioning it out as individual farms ever since. Land is so expensive back East that a lot of church members, especially the younger ones, jumped at the chance to get an affordable farm. That's why we have so many get-togethers during the warmer months to build barns and homes. We're still working on building up the community."

"So people are coming here from all over the country?"

"*Ja*. Just not a lot of single women." He gifted her with a warm smile. "Our bishop is a *gut* man, but there have been times he's had his hands full making sure everything goes smoothly. He'll want to introduce you to everyone after the church service, just so you know, and he usually invites newcomers to meet with him later on so he can get to know them better and understand any concerns or problems they have."

"I see." She wondered what the bishop would think of her.

"There are the Troyers." Matthew pointed toward a buggy approaching a crossroad from another direction. "And behind them is the Chupp family. Everyone's going toward the Stoltzfuses' farm, since they're hosting the service today."

It was a familiar scene for Cara—the growing throng of buggies and people heading toward a common location for worship. She was glad to see it here.

Soon enough Matthew pulled up to a farm with a large house and barn. Women with baskets of food headed toward tables set up under the trees. Men and the older boys took care of the horses. Younger children ran around, often watched by older girls. Cara knew she would be expected to join the women, and suddenly felt lost and shy without Matthew's presence.

Fortunately she saw Miriam Lapp almost immediately. Miriam waved her hand and gestured to join her. Cara nodded and returned the wave.

"I think Miriam just invited me to sit with her in church," she told Matthew as he pulled the buggy to a stop. "I'll take the lunch basket and join her, if you don't mind."

"*Ja*, sure." He smiled. "Don't worry, everyone's looking forward to meeting you."

Cara knew he spoke the truth, but she was glad she had at least one or two acquaintances to shore her up through the day.

She climbed down from the buggy, seized the hamper packed with food and gave Matthew a brave smile before walking into the crowd toward the picnic tables. She was aware of sharpened glances from people as she passed, but no one spoke to her. Socializing happened after church services, not before, so this wasn't unusual.

Fortunately Miriam met her at the table where she was unloading her own basket one-handed as she cradled her baby with the other.

"*Guder mariye,*" Cara greeted. "How is the *boppli* today?"

"Gut." Miriam smiled. "Awkward to be the newcomer at a church service, *ja?*"

"Ja," Cara said in relief, glad Miriam understood.

"You can sit with me. *Komm,* people are starting to be seated."

Cara left the basket on the table, then trailed after Miriam toward the large barn where benches were set up. She filed in and seated herself on the women's side of the room. Plucking up her courage, she looked around at others as they seated themselves, smiling at those who eyed her with curiosity.

"Guder mariye," said a voice. "May I join you?" Anna Miller, Matthew's *mamm,* sidled along the benches.

"Ja sure! *Guder mariye,"* replied Cara, delighted that her future mother-in-law chose to single her out. "It's so *gut* to see you again."

Anna patted Cara's knee in what seemed to be a gesture of affection as she settled herself on the bench. *"Und guder mariye*, Miriam. How's your little *boppli*?"

"*Schön,*" Miriam replied, angling the baby so the older woman could see him more clearly, then resting the infant back over her shoulder.

The service started with hymns familiar to Cara since childhood. Samuel Beiler, the bishop, stood up to offer prayers and scripture readings, and she got her first glimpse of the church leader. He was a lean man in his early sixties, with a long wispy gray beard and kind blue eyes. His voice was powerful and authoritative as he launched into the main sermon. Then came testimonies and closing prayers.

The bishop nodded toward Cara. "I'd like to welcome Cara Lengacher, who is currently Matthew Miller's guest at the boardinghouse. She comes all the way from Pennsylvania."

Knowing it was expected, Cara rose, smiled, nodded, then dropped back into her seat. She heard rustling and low mur-

murs of conversation, and was certain everyone was interpreting the bishop's use of the word "guest" as "future bride." She caught Matthew's eyes from across the room. He winked at her, and she knew he was thinking the same thing.

When the service was over, the chatter started up. Cara filed out of the barn and was soon surrounded by a crowd of women, introducing themselves and inviting her to any number of events—quilting parties and tea socials and knitting circles.

"Danke!" she exclaimed over and over again, knowing she wouldn't be able to keep faces and names straight for some time.

At last Miriam marched over and seized Cara by the arm. "Let her have some lunch!" she said to the other women with a grin, and soon the well-wishers smiled and dispersed.

"Danke," Cara said again, this time to her friend. "They're a friendly group."

"They know you're a mail-order bride," Miriam replied with a bright smile. "I don't know that anyone has even met such a creature, so you're an object of interest at the moment. The hubbub will die down soon enough."

And then start right back up again, thought Cara.

"There's the bishop," said Miriam, nodding toward the church leader striding toward them. "Doubtless he'll want to make an appointment to meet with you privately at some point."

"*Ja,* Matthew said the same thing. *Guder nammidaag,* Bishop," she said more loudly as the elder approached.

"*Guder nammidaag.*" The bishop shook her warmly by the hand. "I'm Samuel Beiler. *Welkom* to our church here in Pierce."

"*Danke.*" Cara kept a pleasant smile on her face. She knew her acceptance into the community depended to a large part on this man's acceptance. "I've had a wonderful *welkom* from everyone so far."

"*Ja*, we're a *gut* group. I wonder if I can invite you to our home for a private chat? My wife and I would like to get to know you better."

"Of course. I'm working all week, but will next Saturday do?"

"Next Saturday is *gut*." The bishop's eyes crinkled with humor. "And my wife, Lois, wanted me to ask you what your favorite type of cookie is so she can be sure to make some."

Cara laughed. "I'm easy. Oatmeal raisin, peanut butter, chocolate chip, anything is fine. What time should I be there?"

"How about two o'clock?"

"Two o'clock will work."

"Enjoy the meal, then." The bishop touched the brim of his straw hat and moved off into the crowd.

"Don't worry," said Miriam, gently propelling Cara toward the tables laden with food. "The bishop is a kind man."

The rest of the afternoon passed pleasantly. Unlike the more structured mealtimes at her old church, people of all ages mixed and ate together. Cara found herself seated next to Matthew and across from Miriam and Aaron, who seemed like an oasis of calm amid the gossip and babble.

Biting into a piece of cold fried chicken, she said, "Three people have asked me so far if I can preserve their garden harvest. Three!"

"And what did you say?" teased Matthew.

"I said *ja*, of course. What else could I say?" Cara chuckled. "They all sounded so apologetic, like they were inconveniencing me. But it's my job. I have a feeling I'll be working nonstop in the next few weeks, since everyone's gardens are being harvested at the same time."

"Well, while you're busy canning, I'll

be busy building a place to put our own canned food." Matthew smiled.

Miriam's eyebrows rose. "What do you mean?"

"It's—it's his wedding present to me," explained Cara, feeling her cheeks heating up. "He's building me the pantry of my dreams."

"Guter mann," pronounced Aaron with a hearty wink toward Matthew. "Give the women what they want."

Cara caught a fast glance between Miriam and Aaron, a subtle exchange of affection that made her swallow hard. Aaron's scarred face was almost unnoticeable when he looked at his wife with such love. It was clear he was crazy about her.

Such affection, she knew, could be hers as well. Matthew practically wore his heart on his sleeve, especially when it came to his enthusiasm about building her a pantry. The love language of men, she knew, often meant they showed their affection with actions, rather than with words.

It was something she had witnessed many times in various couples around her, but never with her parents. Why had her mother married her father? She never knew. They seemed so incompatible.

"Are you okay?" murmured Matthew quietly beside her.

"*Ja,*" Cara replied. "Just thinking about something. I'll tell you about it on the way home."

It warmed her to realize she could trust Matthew to listen to her thoughts. He was such a good man. It was easy to fall in love with him. She hoped—desperately hoped—he would understand when she finally dredged up the courage to tell him the truth of her situation.

"I think everyone enjoyed meeting you today," Matthew said to Cara on the way home. He let Lubelle the horse walk at her own pace since the weather was so pleasant.

"I met so many people, everyone's face was a blur. I will take me a long time to put the names with the faces." She smiled. "But so friendly! For sure and certain I felt very welcomed."

"I know Miriam enjoyed your company."

She sighed. "It's really something, watching Miriam and Aaron together. It's obvious they're crazy about each other."

"*Ja*, it was quite a love story."

"What happened to him? Do you know?"

"He was burned in a barn fire several years ago back in Pennsylvania, and the woman he was courting broke up with him afterward. He moved out here very bitter, and for the longest time he barely left his farm. Then Miriam—who was raised Amish but hadn't been baptized yet—came out from Ohio to visit her brother, hit him with her car on a dark rainy night, and broke his arm. She was so sorry that she took over running his dairy farm while he was recuperating. That's when they fell in love."

Cara's jaw dropped. *"Du machst witze!"* she exclaimed. "That's quite a story!"

"Ain't so? Miriam looks beyond his scars and sees the man beneath. Speaking of which…what were you going to tell me on the way home?"

He saw Cara gaze at the rural landscape, a thoughtful look on her face. "While we were eating the meal with Miriam and Aaron," she said, "I saw this glance of pure affection pass between them. Somehow it made me think of my own parents, and how I never saw anything similar between them. My parents are polite with each other, but hardly affectionate. Then I started wondering why they got married at all, since they never seemed to get along."

He kept his voice gentle. "Are you concerned about the same thing happening to you? Of being trapped in a loveless marriage?"

"Ja und nein," she replied. Her voice sounded strangled, and she cleared it. "I had a brush with that with Andrew, of course, but you're nothing like him. I don't think our marriage will be loveless."

"If you don't mind my asking, why did Andrew leave you?"

She gave an unladylike snort of derision. "Because he found a prettier woman in another Amish community. Or so he said. To be honest, I don't even know if it was true or if he just used it as an excuse to dump me. He moved away and I haven't seen him since. Whatever his excuse, in retrospect I'm glad of it. I don't think we would have been very happy together, and if it wasn't because I had just lost my *grossmammi* at the time, probably I wouldn't have accepted his courtship to begin with."

"So mostly it was your pride that was hurt."

"Ja." Her beautiful eyes crinkled in amusement. "To be fair, I was very interested in using Andrew to get out of my *vater's* house. Maybe at some level he understood that, and that's why he left me."

"Your *daed*… You said he wasn't abusive?"

"Nein, not physically. He never hit *Mamm,* and he never struck us *kinder* except for spanking a bit of childish naughtiness out of us when we were very young. But he's very strict and stern, unyielding and unbending. As the *Englisch* say, it's his way or the highway. Mingled with this was some alleged shame that his youngest daughter wasn't married yet."

"Alleged? What do you mean, alleged?"

"I mean, I wonder how much of that shame was manufactured or if he just wanted me out of the house. When Andrew left me, *Daed* was furious and blamed me, saying I must have done something to drive him away." She sighed. "In short, my home life was a mess, and you can see why I answered your ad in *The Budget*. I—I needed to get away."

"*Ja*, it makes more sense now." He had always taken for granted the strong bond of marital affection between his parents, and credited it for the happy marriages his brothers and sisters had. As the second-to-last unmarried sibling—his younger brother Mark was still single—he yearned for that same level of domestic tranquility.

After a few moments, she asked him, "Why did *you* advertise for a wife in *The Budget*?"

He was silent a moment. "My betrothed also married someone else. We courted for a year before my family moved from Ohio to Montana. I left her with the understanding she would soon follow. She later wrote and said she couldn't bear to leave her family behind and move so far away. I guess courtships don't work long-distance." His hands clenched on the reins as he recalled the anger at receiving her letter. "She left me high and dry. A couple years went by and... I got lonely."

"There was no one local you could court?"

"*Nein.* Supposedly one of the men in church is having his unmarried sister join him here soon to become the settlement's first schoolteacher, but she's not here yet. Quite frankly, I wanted to get married. I prayed long and hard about advertising in *The Budget* and wasn't sure what kind of results I'd get." He smiled at her, admiring anew her beautiful dark eyes, her lovely face. "*Gott* was clearly listening, for how else could He have moved you to answer?"

"It certainly sounds like we both have our reasons." She looked thoughtful, her eyes resting on the horse plodding in front of them. "I hope we can make this work."

"I've heard it said that as long as a couple agrees on three things, they're likely to have a successful marriage," he said.

"What three things?"

"Faith, family, finances. Faith we both have. Family will come. And I don't think you're on a different page regarding finances. I'm confident we'll be very happy together, Cara." He grinned at her. "But remember, out here in Montana, only two of my siblings are here—Eva and Mark. And only Eva has provided my parents with grandkids. You've been warned."

She laughed. "Oh, I'm sure they'll get their grandkids. But I do like your parents. I hope they'll come to accept me. I felt encouraged when your *mamm* chose to sit next to me in church."

"*Ja*, I thought it was a nice sign." Approaching the outskirts of town, he directed the horse toward a side road to avoid traffic on the main street. "I thought about doing some bird-watching this afternoon," he invited. "Are you interested?"

"*Ja*, sure! Speaking of birds, I noticed the bird feeders you have in the backyard of the boardinghouse aren't filled. Why not?"

"Because I want baby birds to learn how to forage for themselves, rather than learning that there's easy food in my backyard. I only feed during the coldest months to keep animals from starving."

"You're a *gut* man, Matthew." The look she gave him was soft and affectionate.

"*Danke.* I hope to prove myself to you and be a *gut hutband.*"

Half an hour later, with the horse stabled and fed, Matthew took a bird book and his one pair of binoculars, and headed for the meandering creek that bordered one edge of the town.

"I wish we had cardinals," he remarked, pointing out a Steller's jay. "Those and fireflies are the two things I miss about Ohio."

"But you say you prefer Montana over-all?"

"Ja." He strolled, the binoculars hanging around his neck. The bird-watching excursion was not so much a scientific expedition as it was an excuse to spend more time in her company. "It's not as humid and not as crowded. And everyone has an opportunity to get a farm if they want it."

"Do you want to have a farm someday?"

"Do you?" He looked at her. "Most church members have an affinity for farming. I don't want to take you away from something you might miss."

"Running a cannery seems incompatible with being a farm wife anyway. No, let's live in town for a few years and see what happens. I may have to give up cannery work once *bopplin* come anyway. If *Gott* wants us to move farther out of town, He'll provide the opportunity."

He was pleased that she seemed so willing to consider a future together, to think about making plans years down the road as a couple.

Daringly he slipped his fingers through hers and felt her return the pressure. "Can you use binoculars with just one hand?" she teased.

"I'd rather hold your hand than watch the birds anyway."

The pressure increased. *"Ich auch,"* she said. "Me too."

For Matthew, it was something akin to a perfect moment. His future with Cara seemed bright. He couldn't possibly see anything that could go wrong or jeopardize what he hoped would be a lifetime of happiness with her.

Chapter Six

Cara glanced at the gauges on the top of the massive pressure canners bubbling on the propane burners. Three of the huge canners held fifty-seven quarts of spicy marinara sauce, which would be sold in the Yoders' store. The fourth canner held nineteen jars of ground beef, the beginning of her own collection of canned food to be stored in the pantry Matthew was building.

The canners were at her favorite stage—the sweet spot when the pressure was holding at just the right level—but habit made her check the gauges every couple of minutes to make sure the pressure wasn't dipping too low or moving too high. The batch of ground beef alone needed to be processed at fifteen pounds of pressure for ninety minutes, and until it was finished, she wouldn't leave her post for more than a minute or two. Vigilance was crucial.

It was the Monday morning after her first church service, and the weather had turned rainy and blustery, with a chill indicating that winter wasn't far away. To her way of thinking, it was perfect canning weather. She could hear the soothing sound of intermittent rain showers on the roof overhead, and through the tall, narrow windows of the building, gray light came in, making the cannery feel very industrial and efficient.

She was alone in the facility. Matthew was back at the boardinghouse checking in some new guests, and the Yoders were busy in the store.

She resumed her task of peeling carrots—beginning the process of preserving Miriam's garden harvest—when an *Englisch* woman walked in through the connecting door from the Yoders' store. She was middle-aged, perhaps early 60s, and a bit plump, with a pleasant smile and a dripping umbrella.

"Good morning," she said. "The man in the store said I should talk to you about a canning project."

"Good morning," Cara replied. "*Ja*, I'm the new canning expert. What did you have in mind?"

"I had a bumper crop in my garden this year," the woman explained. "I wanted to know if I could use this facility to do some canning."

"Hmm." Cara laid down her peeler. "I think the understanding for this facility is I would be doing all the work. Letting someone else use it might be an issue of liability for the Yoders, who own it. But if you wait here a moment, let me go get Mabel Yoder and you can ask her."

She snatched up a dish towel and wiped her hands as she headed into the mercantile. Mabel was alone at the cash register. "There's an *Englischer* in the cannery who has a question I can't answer," she told the older woman. "Can you come over?"

"Can't answer?" Mabel chuckled as she followed Cara. "I thought you knew everything about canning."

The *Englisch* woman hadn't moved, and was glancing around the facility with interest. Cara considered this a good sign. People unfamiliar with such workspaces often became annoying by poking around where they had no business going. Cara glanced at the gauges on the pressure canners, then said to Mabel, "This lady would like to use the facility's resources to can her own garden harvest. I wasn't sure of the liability factor, so that's why I needed your input."

"I see." Mabel glanced at the woman

thoughtfully. "What is it you wanted to can up?"

"Oh, all kinds of things," said the *Englischer.* "Green beans, carrots, corn, that kind of thing. I've canned before," she added defensively. "I know what I'm doing. But I had such an abundant harvest that I thought it would be easier to process it in a larger facility rather than my small kitchen. I have my own jars and lids, and I'm perfectly willing to pay for the time it would take me to process everything."

Mabel rubbed her chin. "We had thought to open the cannery to the public in the future for just the kinds of projects you're talking about, but at the moment we need to get one or two more permits to do so legally."

"What about this?" suggested Cara. "This lady—I'm sorry, I don't know your name..."

"Lucy," the woman replied. "Lucy Naylor."

"I'm Cara Lengacher," replied Cara with a smile, before turning back to Mabel. "What about if Lucy processed her harvest under my supervision?"

"I suppose that would work..." Mabel sounded hesitant.

Lucy Naylor smiled. "That would be fine with me. I see you have some wonderfully large water-bath pots for processing jars, much larger than I have, so it won't take very long..."

"But you're not using the water-bath pots for carrots or green beans or corn," interrupted Cara. She gestured to the massive pressure canners gently bubbling on the propane stovetop. "You'll need to pressure-can them."

"No, I don't bother with that. I've never owned a pressure canner. I use a water bath for all my vegetables."

Alarm bells sounded inside Cara's head. Vegetables were low-acid. Low-acid foods needed to be pressure canned. If low-acid foods were processed in a water bath, there was a high likelihood the food could be contaminated with deadly botulism spores. That was the oldest rule in the canning book when it came to the safe processing of food.

"No," she snapped. "Absolutely not."

"What?" Lucy looked startled. "What do you mean, 'no'?"

"I mean, you can't water-bath vegetables. They have to be processed in a pressure canner to be safe from botulism."

"Oh, botulism." Lucy gave a dismissive wave of her hand. "That's overhyped. I've been canning in water baths for years and have never gotten botulism."

"Past performance is no guarantee of future results," Cara quoted with some asperity. "I'm sorry, Mrs. Naylor, but I will not permit you to engage in unsafe canning practices in this facility. However, I would be happy to process your harvest for you."

"You're just being picky," snapped Lucy, crossing her arms on her chest.

"My granny canned in a water bath for decades and the food was always fine."

Cara resisted the urge to snap, "Then your granny was a fool." She took a breath, glanced at the pressure gauges, then shook her head. "The answer is still no. Ma'am, you have to understand—it's basic canning science. Only high-acid foods can be processed in a water bath. Perhaps you can do a bit more research to confirm that."

"I think you're being unreasonable." Lucy drew herself up in a huff. "I'm sorry to have wasted your time." Scowling, she stalked out of the cannery and disappeared through the connecting door to the mercantile.

Cara exhaled and glanced at Mabel, who stood rooted, staring after the woman. "I'm sorry. I hope I didn't lose a customer for you, but there's no way I can stand by and let someone engage in something so dangerous, especially in this facility. I hope you're not angry with me."

"Angry?" Mabel turned a smiling face upon her. "On the contrary, I'm impressed! I'm not the expert canner you are, but even I know you're not supposed to process vegetables in a water bath. That's why I'm confident about selling your products in our store—I know they're safe."

Cara dropped down onto the high wooden stool she sometimes used while peeling vegetables. "Matthew suggested I might teach canning classes at some point." She gestured toward the unfinished side of the building. "Maybe I should take him up on that. It simply drives me *nuts* to have someone dismiss the dangers of botulism."

"Have you ever known anyone who got botulism?"

"Not personally, no. My *grossmammi*, who first taught me to can, was something of a formidable force in my old town. She was a *gut* influence on the younger women, making sure everyone understood the correct way to do things."

Mabel patted Cara on the shoulder. "I'm glad you're carrying on your *grossmammi's* wisdom. Don't worry if this woman doesn't come back. I'm not bothered by that. You can't please everyone." She headed back toward the store.

Cara glanced at the pressure gauges, then checked the kitchen timers she used to keep track of how long to process the food. Only ten more minutes and she could turn off the heat and let the canners gradually cool down. Only when the internal pressure registered zero would she remove the jars from the canner to the cooling racks, then listen to the sweet sound of the lids sealing, one by one, with a melodious pop.

Canning was a wondrous method of food preservation. She had thought so since she was five years old and her grandmother first taught her the safe way to preserve tomatoes. Now, as an adult, she realized she had adopted her grandmother's mission to make sure others understood the necessary safety rules.

She sighed and returned to peeling carrots. She hoped Lucy Naylor would do some research and conclude that she should, indeed, take food safety seriously.

"You look like you have a thundercloud overhead," observed Matthew.

She whipped her head up and smiled. "I didn't hear you come in. *Ja*, actually the thundercloud just huffed her way out of the store." She related the incident with Lucy Naylor. "I tell you, Matthew, it was all I could do to keep my temper. Why is it that the more wrong people are, the more arrogant they are about their lack of knowledge?"

He chuckled. "So my future bride has a temper?"

"Sometimes." She grinned. "When my buttons are pushed. And this woman pushed them pretty hard. Now, I fear, she's going to go home and process her green beans in a water bath, and I pray she doesn't land herself or her *hutband* in the hospital ill from botulism."

"Why do I think the best thing Abe and Mabel ever did was to hire you?" He leaned over and dropped a light kiss on her cheek.

She felt her face heat up at the unexpected kiss. "It's all part of *Gott's* plan," she told him. Daringly, since no one was around, she looped her arms loosely around his neck. "I'm just so happy to be here."

Matthew spent a happy afternoon working the same room as Cara. While she worked on pressure-canning various items, he cut insulation and stapled them to studs. They kept up a running conversation across the width of the large space.

"Did you know that Aaron is an inventor?"

"Aaron? No, Miriam never mentioned it." Cara paused as she lifted jars into the canner. "He's a man of many talents for sure and certain."

"*Ja*, he's a clever fellow. He invented a small hand-powered milking machine that got picked up by a manufacturer a couple years ago and is selling very well. He also has a number of other little farm devices he's developed over time. And he's the settlement's best cheese-maker. He sells his cheese through the Yoders' store."

"And Miriam is a midwife. Talented pair, both of them." She settled more jars into the canner and lifted the heavy lid into place.

"*Ja*. There's a lot of talent in our church. A few years ago, the town leaders went to the bishop and asked if the church would put on a demonstration for the town's Mountain Days festival. They wanted us to showcase our collective talent. I suspect they also wanted to satisfy the curiosity of the *Englisch*, since our church was still new in the area and the locals were largely unfamiliar with Amish culture."

"That same curiosity contributes to the whole tourist industry back East."

"*Ja*, but here it's not so bad. The bishop was anxious to have good relations with the *Englischers* in town. The town has been very supportive of us, including such things as installing hitching posts in various areas."

"That's *gut*, then."

"*Ja.* It was a tremendous success, and the Amish community has participated in the festival ever since."

"The Yoders seem to stock a lot of products made by us, too."

"Almost everything in the store is Amish-made. That's why they were so interested in establishing a cannery, and now a bakery. They're clever business-people, for sure and certain."

"At least the tourism isn't so bad." She sighed. "The last cannery I worked at was in the midst of a tourist village near Lancaster. Busloads of people would come every day to gawp at us Amish. As annoying as it is to feel like an animal in a zoo, there was no doubt a lot of people in our district were able to make a living by selling their crafts and quilts. With farmland becoming so scarce, many had no choice but to cater to *Englisch* tourists."

"That's why I suspect our church in Pierce will just be the first of several more church districts in Montana," said Matthew as he sliced open another bundle of insulation. "Most people want to farm, but what can you do if there's no farmland? So many *youngies* have to work among the *Englisch* simply to earn a living, and I know that church leaders are worried about the temptations."

"So it's a chance for a new start, here in Montana." It was a statement, not a question.

"*Ja.* During the meal after yesterday's service, if you were to ask anyone why they came out here, most would say it had to do with land prices. I have a feeling church leaders back East are now keeping an eye on the Western real estate market, watching for another huge plot of land to come up for sale. But of course, the ranchland has to be suitable for farming of some sort. There's a lot of dry scrubland in the eastern part of the state that isn't much good except for range cattle. So it's a balance."

"What are your goals, Matthew?" Cara took up a knife and began slicing corn kernels from cobs. "You mentioned you were fine living in town for a while, but you also mentioned the possibility of taking over your parents' farm at some point. Which do you prefer? Do you want to farm?"

"Sometimes it's hard to say." He fit another batt of insulation in place. "There are advantages to both. Right now the boardinghouse is pulling in enough income to support me. I mean, *us*." He flashed her a grin. "And the extra carpentry work the Yoders provide is just gravy. But my parents aren't getting any younger, and since my brother Mark already has his own farm, it's likely I'll take over my parents' land when *Daed* wants to retire. In that case perhaps we can find a manager for the boardinghouse."

"Lots of options, then."

"*Ja.* And I'm grateful you're willing to be flexible about our future, whether it's living in town or on the farm."

She shrugged, keeping her eyes on the knife in her hand as she sliced the corn. "If the last year has taught me nothing else, it's taught me how to roll with the punches."

There was a grim note to her voice that startled him. Matthew knew she'd had a tough year, but he had the uneasy feeling there was something deeper to her statement. Was there something she wasn't telling him? Well, he could hardly pry every single secret out of her in the short amount of time they'd known each other.

The best he could do was let her know he was always willing to listen. Hopefully, whatever was bothering her would come out at some point.

He wasn't sure whether to feel annoyed or not by this realization. He'd been as up-front and honest with her as he could be. He wanted all their cards laid on the table before they joined their lives together. Was it too much to ask her to do the same?

He was anxious to get married, yet something inside him was telling him to slow down. He was courting Cara, sure, but perhaps it was best if the courtship were to last another year rather than rushing to get married in November.

And yet...if she *was* hiding something, how bad could it be? He knew she had spent her whole life within her church. She hadn't left during her *rumspringa*. She was baptized. While her family life sounded rough, there was no indication of misbehavior, no hint of scandal.

Maybe he was imagining things, over-thinking and over analyzing every tone of voice or toss-away comment. The fact was, he didn't *want* to discover anything bad about her. He wanted to fall in love with her, get married, start a family and live happily ever after. Was that too much to ask?

Chapter Seven

Walking toward Bishop Beiler's home, Cara was armed with a simple map Matthew had hand-drawn for her so she could find it.

"Are you sure you don't want me to drive you in the buggy?" he had offered.

But she'd declined, claiming she needed the exercise. "Since I'm in the cannery all day, a walk will do me some good."

In truth, she needed the solitude to prepare herself to deceive the church leader about her condition. She rested her hand on her midsection, feeling the gentle swell of her unborn child. She was still barely showing, and had merely loosened the ties of her apron a bit. No one could even claim she was merely plump, at least not yet. Because she was on the tall side, her condition wasn't obvious…except to her.

In the mirror, her face seemed fuller than normal, but again she doubted anyone else would notice. Nor had she felt any morning sickness, though she was starting to feel fatigued by the end of the day in the cannery.

How long could she pull this off?

It took her about an hour to get to the Beilers' home, which looked like a repurposed barn with a wide lawn in front. A large vegetable garden, fenced tall against deer, was in front next to the lawn. Cara walked up the porch steps and knocked on the door, discreetly wiping her damp palms on her apron.

A short plump woman, her gray hair tucked neatly under her *kapp*, answered. "*Guten tag.* You must be Cara Lengacher. I'm Lois Beiler."

"*Guten tag.* So nice to meet you at last." Cara shook hands with her.

"*Komm* in, *komm* in." Lois stepped aside to usher Cara into the house to their comfortable living room.

The bishop emerged from another room. "*Guten tag,* Cara," he rumbled. "You walked here, I assume? Have a seat."

Lois disappeared into the kitchen for a moment, then emerged bearing a tray laden with tea along with a platter of homemade oatmeal raisin cookies. She placed the tray on the coffee table by the chairs. "Mabel Yoder is so delighted that you're operating the cannery, child," she said as she poured the beverage. "She couldn't be more pleased that you're here."

Cara felt herself relax. The bishop and his wife were an agreeable couple. They were certainly not out to trap her into confessing her sin. No, this was nothing more than a pleasant social visit.

"I couldn't be more pleased to be there,"

she said. "Has Mabel told you about my qualifications?"

"*Nein.*" Lois shook her head.

Cara gave a brief summary of her work history, then outlined her goals for the cannery. "I have about a hundred recipes from the last cannery where I worked," she told the Beilers. "Everything from salad dressings to fruit butters to chutneys to food dips, in addition to every jam and jelly recipe under the sun. I made a batch of peach salsa that sold out in one day. Once the townspeople understand they can get a different item each day, I think that section of the store will become very popular."

"And what about canning garden produce?" inquired Lois. She gestured toward the kitchen. "I'm in the middle of canning myself."

"*Ja*, it's the busiest time of year for that," admitted Cara. "Miriam Lapp was the first to ask if I could preserve her garden harvest, since she has the new baby, but she's not the only one. Mabel already said it's better to concentrate on preserving the harvest than selling anything in the store right now, since the cannery is meant to be a service to church members above all. I can make things to sell in the store the rest of the year."

"The Yoders are smart businesspeople," remarked the bishop. "None better. And they do everything possible to benefit the church members while serving the community. Now—" the bishop took a sip of tea "—tell me how things are between you and Matthew. Being a mail-order bride must be an unnerving experience, *ja*?"

"*Ja*." Cara decided to be as truthful as possible—with one major exception, of course. "I did not know what to expect when I met him at the boardinghouse, but I'm delighted. He's a kind man, Bishop Beiler, and after what I left behind in Dufflebug, Pennsylvania, I couldn't be more delighted." She told him about her rocky

family life and the humiliation of Andrew's desertion. "By contrast, Matthew
is rock-solid," she concluded. Hesitating
a moment, she then added, "I understand
his parents were against him advertising
for a wife, but I've done my best to make
a *gut* impression with them. I hope Matthew doesn't suffer any repercussions by
courting me."

The bishop stroked his wispy beard. "I
suspect they'll come around. It's not like
them to be so…*rigid* about something like
this. There may be something behind it
I'm not aware of. As for Matthew—well,
I haven't talked to him privately since
your arrival, but at last week's church service, he certainly had the look of a happy
man."

"That makes two of us. To be honest,
Bishop, I've been thanking *Gott* daily for
His hand in connecting Matthew and me
through the advertisement."

"Matthew has always enjoyed a high
standing within the church ever since

he arrived in Montana," confirmed the bishop. "While he raised a few eyebrows at his technique for finding a bride, no one had any doubt he would make some woman an excellent *hutband*. He's hard-working, straightforward and—as you point out—kind."

"That attitude is something I value very much," Cara said as she sipped her tea. "I see no obstacle to a November wedding."

"Ah, the wedding." The bishop reached for a cookie. "Since no one knows better than you the importance of not being joined in haste lest you repent at leisure, I urge you to consider spending the next year getting better acquainted with Matthew, and target *next* November for your wedding. A longer courtship is always recommended, especially since you started out as strangers to each other."

"Is that a requirement?" asked Cara. "Because Matthew indicated getting married this November is fine with him."

"Did he?" The bishop's bushy eyebrows

rose. "Well, if you are both in agreement, I have no objection—though I would still counsel delay. What difference does it make whether it's this year or next, as long as you know you have each other?"

The difference is a baby, thought Cara, but of course could not say it out loud. Besides, regardless of the year, she knew she could not deceive Matthew going into the marriage. Before November, she would have to tell him the truth.

"I'll talk things over again with Matthew," she countered, giving the bishop and his wife a cheerful smile. "I think Matthew is anxious to get married, or at least that's the impression I got. If he prefers not to wait, I have no objection either."

"Ja gut," replied the bishop, though he gave her a questioning look. "My wife has a lot of celery in the garden, for whenever the wedding takes place," he joked.

Cara laughed outright. Celery had a rich and nuanced meaning at Amish weddings.

Not only was it often the only plant still showing leafy greenery during November, but its presence hinted subtly at fertility. Abundant celery planted in someone's garden during the summer was often a silent announcement about a young person's wedding plans in November.

"I'm glad to hear it," she replied, "since I have no family here to provide it, and Matthew doesn't have much more than an herb garden in the back of the boardinghouse."

The moment of levity seemed to erase any concerns from the church leader and his wife. The visit ended with additional words of welcome and well wishes, and Lois pressed a container of oatmeal cookies in Cara's hands to share with Matthew back at the boardinghouse.

Cara walked slowly back toward town. The day was crisp and fall-like, and she wondered what the winters were like in this part of the country.

If she was here to see the winter. Matthew would learn soon enough that she carried another man's child, and there was a large chance he would reject her. Could she stay here in Pierce without his support? The immediacy of when she must tell him was starting to gnaw at her.

And yet…she found she was reluctant to disturb the growing friendship between her and Matthew. He was more than a means to rescue her from the disgrace of an out-of-wedlock pregnancy. He was fast becoming a truly welcome groom-to-be, someone trustworthy and dependable. Everyone she had met so far in Pierce—Abe and Mabel Yoder, Miriam and Aaron Lapp, and now Bishop Beiler and his wife—spoke very highly of him. Now that she was getting to know him, she understood why.

He represented everything she had always wanted in her life—the blessing of a peaceful domestic life with a *hutband* whom she could love and support. He was more, far more, than she'd anticipated as a result of answering an ad in *The Budget*.

The thought of tipping over the apple cart was worrying indeed.

She placed her hand on her midsection. The tiny person growing within her was innocent of any of the drama taking place in Cara's world.

She didn't know what the future held... only that she knew it would involve bearing her child in a new community far away from her hometown. Matthew might renounce her when he learned the truth, and she wouldn't blame him. What might happen after that was anyone's guess.

All she could do was pray to *Gott* for guidance.

Matthew stacked firewood with efficient movements, placing it in neat rows in an open-sided, covered shed near the stable where he kept the horse. His brother-in-law Daniel had a side business selling firewood, and Matthew routinely purchased several cords each fall to heat the boardinghouse through the cold winter months.

While each room in the boardinghouse had its own propane wall heater, Matthew far preferred the warmth of wood heat in both the lobby of the building as well as his private quarters. Since the rented rooms weren't occupied at all times, it made sense not to have a heating system for the whole building. Besides, wood heat provided warmth even during power outages, and most people in town—even the *Englisch*—had an alternate heat source for just such occasions.

It felt good to use his muscles. He sometimes feared he would get out of shape by not working a farm, so he welcomed any opportunity for physical labor—doing carpentry or helping his *daed* plow a field or, in this case, stacking firewood.

While he worked, he wondered how the meeting between Cara and the bishop was going. It wasn't that the church leader was intimidating, exactly, but the elder undoubtedly commanded respect. His wife, Lois, acted as a gentler counterpart to her husband's ministerial duties, offering sweetness and sympathy when needed. Between them, they made a formidable team.

Lois Beiler's presence, he knew, would put Cara at her ease, rather than having an intimidating tête-à-tête with the church leader by himself. This was, after all, a social call rather than a counseling session or a reprimand.

He stacked more wood higher against the shed wall. He himself had never had a meeting with the bishop except purely social ones. He had never required spiritual counseling or received a reprimand of any sort. He sometimes wondered about those discussions. What took place behind the closed doors? What words of wisdom did the elder say to keep people on the straight and narrow? Matthew honestly didn't know.

"I'm back."

Whirling around, he saw Cara standing behind him, a shy smile on her face. She looked lovely, with her cheeks flushed from the walk and her dark eyes filled with an unfathomable expression. She held a plastic container in one hand.

"Welkom," he said. He removed his work gloves, fished a handkerchief from his back pocket and wiped his face. "How did the meeting go?"

"It was fine. The Beilers are very nice people." She lifted the bag up. "Lois sent oatmeal cookies."

"That was thoughtful."

"Do you need help?" she added, eyeing the pile of unstacked wood on the ground.

"Ja, if you want to. I have another pair of gloves in the stable." He fetched the pair and handed it to her. "So, what did you talk about with the bishop?"

She picked up some cordwood and

began stacking. "A lot of it was just learning who I am. I told him about my family back in Pennsylvania, and what happened with my former fiancé, and the reasons why I answered your ad for a bride in *The Budget*. I also let him know about the cannery where I used to work. And of course, he wanted to know about our future plans."

"I suspected as much." He grinned at her.

She smiled back. "He thinks the world of you, Matthew. He had nothing but praise for you, and what an upstanding a member of the church you are."

"That's *gut*, then." While the approval from the church leader was welcome, Matthew felt a moment's unease. Praise was not usually encouraged within the Amish community, where expected behavior was reinforced through more nuanced and subtle means of peer pressure rather than overt words. "What else did he say?"

"He wanted to know our wedding plans, of course. He urged us to wait until next November so we can get to know each other better, though to be honest I think I'd rather get married this November. However he said the decision will ultimately depend on you. That is to say, we both need to agree."

"I'm fine either way," he said. "But why do you prefer this November rather than waiting?"

She kept her eyes on the wood she was stacking. "I see no reason to wait," she replied.

"Are you sure you're willing take a chance on me?" He tried to keep his tone light.

She leveled a look at him, her dark eyes serious. "The bishop says you're a *gut* man. Everything I've learned about you reinforces that. Why should I want to wait?"

"Well, if you're sure…" He paused a moment, and eyed the remaining pile of split wood on the ground. "I think we can finish this another time, *ja*? I'm ready for some dinner. I'm as hungry as a horse."

In reality it wasn't the dinner he wanted so much as he had something he wanted to show her.

He followed her inside the building and behind the check-in desk toward his private quarters. The unfinished pantry loomed up, right next to the kitchen.

Suddenly stopping in her tracks, she exclaimed, "You've made progress!"

He chuckled. "I wanted to surprise you."

The food storage room was little more than a skeletal structure, but its exact dimensions were much more apparent to his soon-to-be bride. He walked into the structure with her. "I took to heart your admiration for my *mamm's* flour sifter," he said, and pointed to a framed-in shape. "I can get a sturdy metal flour sifter from a place I know back East, and install it in here. The kind I'm thinking about holds about twenty-five pounds of flour. By having it here, at the end of the freestanding center shelves, it will be easily accessible from the kitchen."

Cara's eyes were glowing as she took in his handiwork. Matthew felt a swell of pride that she was pleased with his gift.

"Oh, Matthew..." She gave him a quick hug. "You're so *gut* to me."

He returned the embrace for a few moments before reluctantly pulling away. "What do you say to pizza tonight for dinner?" he inquired. "I have some fresh mozzarella Aaron made."

"Sounds *wunderbar*!" Comfortable in the kitchen now, Cara began assembling the ingredients needed to make the pizza dough. She chattered as she mixed and kneaded it, while Matthew grated the cheese and sliced onions.

These were the moments Matthew treasured—when they worked together on mutual projects, even something as mundane as stacking firewood or making a meal. He had never had such a routine with a woman before. Each evening Cara helped tidy the kitchen, thanked him for the meal she'd helped prepare, then departed for her solitary room. He would go about closing down the boardinghouse for the night, making sure any guests had whatever they needed, then return to his own quarters.

Now that he had tasted the contrast—the company of a compatible woman—he wanted more. He wanted to sit opposite her in the comfortable living room chairs, reading or discussing the day's events. In the winter, warmed by the wood cookstove straddling the kitchen and living room, he looked forward to seeing her working at the jigsaw puzzles she'd said she enjoyed doing, shelving her favorite books on the bookshelves he planned to build on the outside wall of the pantry, and otherwise personalizing these rooms to be hers as well as his.

And, hopefully someday, making space for *kinder*...

"Tomorrow is a visiting Sunday," he remarked as they ate their pizza. "Since there's no church, what do you say to walking over to visit my sister Eva and her *hutband* Daniel? You met them briefly after church last Sunday, but she was busy with her toddler. You'll like Eva," he added. "She's one of the most popular women in the church for being so kind and down-to-earth."

"If she's anything like you, I'm not surprised." Cara sipped her glass of sun tea. "That's one thing I'm coming to realize— how solid and well-liked your family is here in Pierce. You, your parents, now your sister and brother-in-law. You have one other brother here, *ja*?"

"*Ja*, Mark is his name." Matthew chuckled. "He's been very interested in how you and I are getting along since he's also single. I don't think it ever occurred to him to advertise for a wife, but short of going back East to court someone, he may have to try the same thing."

"What a pity I don't have an unmarried sister," she remarked. "Sadly, I don't think I have anyone I can recommend for him, either. I had no idea single women were in such high demand out here."

"*Ja*, it's almost like pioneer days, ain't so? A woman could have her choice of men." He smiled at her. "I'm just grateful to *Gott* you chose me."

She cast her eyes down in apparent shyness. "I am too," she said in a low voice.

"About November, then..." He paused and took the plunge. "We can go talk to the bishop this week and confirm we both are in agreement for a November wedding."

"*Danke!*" Her eyes glowed and she smiled that wonderful smile that never failed to weaken his knees. "I'm looking forward to doing this every night with you—making dinner, washing dishes, reading..."

So it wasn't just him who thought about the joys of domestic life in his mind. Matthew dropped any concerns he was having. If she was looking forward to the exact same thing he was in married life, then surely they were made for each other, ain't so?

Chapter Eight

Visiting Sundays were pleasant times characterized by no work and lots of socializing. Without a worship service, it was a chance to strengthen social bonds and community ties in a low-key and relaxed environment.

Lying in bed that morning, Cara found herself feeling somewhat desperate rather than relaxed. It had nothing to do with visiting Matthew's sister and brother-in-law. Instead, she was thinking about how the bishop had been urging her to postpone the wedding for another year. She was just glad Matthew had agreed to an earlier wedding date.

She touched her abdomen. So far she had felt no movement, no sign of life from the baby within her, but she had surreptitiously brought a book on pregnancy in her luggage which confirmed everything was developing normally. She was about ten weeks along. According to her reading, the baby's arms, hands, fingers, feet and toes were fully formed. But it was too soon to feel any kicking. It still seemed unreal somehow, yet she knew it was very real.

What to do about the wedding? Or more importantly, when should she tell Matthew? Of course, there was every likelihood there would be no wedding—this year or next—once he learned of her condition. Even if they married in November, she couldn't trick him into thinking the baby was his. She would be almost four months along by the time the wedding came about. For another, she couldn't do that to such a decent and honorable man as Matthew. She might be desperate, but she wasn't cruel.

So she must tell him at some point. The question was, when?

After praying about it, she finally decided on a course of action: She must convince Matthew that she was a good match despite her pregnancy. She would charm him, be more affectionate with him, and encourage him to fall in love with her more than she knew he already was. She would embark on a quest to win him over completely, and then—well in advance of the wedding—drop the bombshell. She would also explain the circumstances how she became pregnant.

Thus resolved, she rose, washed and dressed. Descending the stairs to the lobby, she could hear small noises and movements in the kitchen, and smiled to herself. Doubtless Matthew was making omelets, something he often did for breakfast. The connecting door was open as it often was in the morning, so he could listen for the service bell and check out or assist any guests.

He was using the wood cookstove, for the morning was chilly. She saw a tray of biscuits, already baked, resting on the warming shelf. Matthew was grating some cheese.

"Guder mariye," she greeted him.

He lifted his head and smiled. *"Guder mariye,"* he returned. "A blessed Sunday to you."

"Dunke. Same to you. What can I do to help?"

"Perhaps chop up some onions? I've got everything else ready for the omelets."

He knew what she liked by now, and since his tastes were similar, he simply made the same thing for her.

"I'm looking forward to visiting your sister today," she said. "How many children does she have?"

"Four. Miriam delivered her last one, little Eli. He's two years old now." He smiled at her. "I'm looking forward to having my own *bopplin* someday."

Sooner than you think, she thought to herself, but instead she merely smiled, making sure to add a bit of flirtatiousness to her expression.

After washing the breakfast dishes, Matthew hitched up the horse and buggy. "They live about four miles away," he said. "I've walked it, but it's a bit far."

"*Ja,* I won't argue." She donned a cloak and allowed Matthew to assist her into the buggy.

Matthew pulled on a coat, then climbed into the seat and took the reins. Within moments, the horse was trotting toward the edge of town. "Chilly this morning," he observed. "Not quite freezing, though, so people can still do some late harvesting from their gardens."

"When does this area see its first snowfall?"

"Sometimes in late October, but more

often in November. This day will warm up into sparkling sunshine, just you watch."

He pointed out various landmarks as they moved deeper into the Amish settlement, noting who lived where as they passed farmhouses. "And here's my sister's home," he concluded.

The Hostetler house was a handsome two-story structure with a fenced yard "to keep the kids in," Matthew joked, as he pulled up alongside the gate.

Almost immediately a pretty woman with a strong physical resemblance to Matthew spilled out onto the porch, holding a toddler in her arms. A man stepped out behind her.

"Welkom, welkom!" the woman called. As Cara climbed out of the buggy, Eva walked down the path to greet her. "I'm so happy you came to visit!"

The moment Cara came through the gate, Eva placed her toddler on the ground and embraced Cara like she was a long-lost sister. "I didn't have a chance to chat with you after church last week, and I've felt terrible about it ever since," she explained. "Matthew's been talking about you long before you even arrived in Pierce. Oh, this is my *hutband*, Daniel."

Cara reached over to shake hands with the man, but Eva monopolized her. "*Komm* inside, I have tea and cookies all set out," she said. She grabbed her toddler and swung him back on her hip. "I've been looking forward to this! I can't tell you how happy I was to learn Matthew was getting married."

"Matthew, I could use your help in the barn carrying a coffee table I just repaired into the house," Daniel said to Matthew.

Before she knew it, Cara had been introduced to Eva's four children, given a quick tour of the house, and invited to help herself to some cookies while Eva poured tea. The men, meanwhile, had disappeared outside, walking toward an outbuilding.

"How are you liking everyone here in Pierce?" asked Eva, sipping her tea.

"Very much," replied Cara. "I'm sure Matthew has filled you in on what my life was like back in Pennsylvania, and why I was anxious to move away. But honestly, Eva, I have been so happy since coming here. I've met your parents, and I liked them a lot. And now to have a sister here as well…"

Eva gave her hand a quick squeeze before reaching down to pull her sleepy toddler, Eli, into her lap. She cuddled the boy and rocked a bit in chair, her movements confident and experienced. "I miss my own sisters," she said. "They're back in Ohio. We write as often as we can, of course, but it's not the same as having them just down the road. You're to visit as often as you can, do you hear?" she added in a mock-severe tone.

Cara laughed. "I don't want to be a bother."

"Family are never a bother."

"So how did you and Daniel end up here in Montana?"

"It was *Daed* who talked us into it," Eva replied. "Daniel was working construction, but he wasn't happy. He wanted a farm, and farmland was simply too expensive in Ohio. When we caught wind of this new settlement, *Daed* talked the three of us into coming with him. He sold his property in Ohio, and with the money he was able to purchase not just the boardinghouse, but their very own farm. Mark—that's my other brother—and Daniel snapped up land of their own, and Matthew decided to try managing the boardinghouse." Eva cocked her head. "Do you mind living in town?"

"Matthew's asked me that a number of times. *Nein,* for the moment I'm fine with it, especially since I'm getting the cannery up and running. Oh, Eva, you have no idea how nice it is to have such a beautiful little facility to work in!" She glanced around the kitchen. "Do you can?"

"*Ja*, of course. And yes, I'm doing it properly," she added with a twinkle in her eye. "*Mamm* taught me right. But I know some old-timers who insist on water-bath canning their beans."

"*Ja*, I met an *Englischer* the other day who got huffy with me when I wouldn't let her use the cannery to do the same thing. Fortunately Mabel was there and backed me up, *Gott* bless her."

Little Eli had fallen asleep on his mother's shoulder, lulled by the chatter and the warm kitchen. Cara looked at the child's rosy cheeks and innocent face, and her throat threatened to close up. Soon enough she would be holding her own little one like that...but whether she would be chatting across the table with Matthew's sister while doing so was not clear.

Eva was as lovable and friendly as Cara could ever hope for in a sister-in-law. But how would she feel about her brother marrying someone who was already expecting another man's baby?

Fortunately, such dire thoughts were interrupted when Matthew and Daniel came inside, carrying a pine table between them, with a leg clearly mended. Matthew bumped the front door closed behind him, then the men placed the table in the living room among some easy chairs.

"So who was jumping on the table?" he asked his sister with a twinkle in his eye.

"Jacob, who else?" she replied. "That child has the energy of two *kinder*. Daniel said he would start teaching him carpentry to calm him down."

Listening to the loving and casual conversation between family members, Cara felt a pang of longing. How dearly she wanted this family to be hers too.

But could they accept the baggage she'd brought along with her from Pennsylvania?

* * *

Matthew watched the dawning friendship between his future wife and his sister, and smiled with satisfaction. He suspected Cara could use a friend, and both Eva and Miriam had reached out to Cara. He was pleased.

"…in the store?" asked Cara.

He blinked. "I'm sorry, I was woolgathering. What did you say?"

"I said, have you heard Eva is going to be selling her baby quilts in the Yoders' store?" Cara pointed to a small quilt draped over the back of one of the kitchen chairs.

"Since when?" Matthew asked his sister.

"Since last week," she replied over the head of her sleeping son. "Mabel finally convinced me."

"Nothing about your drawings?" Daniel said in a teasing voice.

"Of course not," Eva answered pertly. "That would be *hochmut*."

"Drawings?" inquired Cara. "Are you an artist?"

"*Nein*, not at all. But I have a little bit of skill with a pencil."

Daniel gave a mock-derisive snort. "Let me show you an example of her 'little bit of skill.'" He reached into a Hoosier cabinet and withdrew a small framed item.

Cara took it in her hands while Matthew peered over her shoulder. It was a pencil sketch of quilts hanging from a clothesline, flapping in an invisible breeze.

"Beautiful," breathed Cara.

"*Ja, schwester,*" Matthew teased. "Not bad."

"Why don't you hang this on the wall?" asked Cara, handing the drawing back.

"*Hochmut,*" Eva said simply. "It's just a little hobby I enjoy, but no need to show it off."

"But you could earn some extra money selling these in the Yoders' store too," urged Cara.

"I've told her that," Daniel said, smiling at his wife. "But she refuses."

"Besides," said Eva, gently patting her sleeping son on the back. "They already have an artist whose work is on display."

"I've seen some artwork in the store," said Cara. "But I thought they were painted by an *Englischer*."

"*Nein,* the artist used to be an *Englischer*, but she's Amish now. Her name is Penelope Troyer, and she's married to a man in our church who runs a B and B on the edge of the settlement. She's a *real* artist, not an amateur like me."

"It's another example of the collective talent within our church," said Matthew. "No wonder the Mountain Days Amish demonstrations are so popular."

"*Ja,* because Eva's baby quilts are the best in the settlement." Daniel leaned down and placed a smacking kiss on his wife's cheek.

"This is *wunnerschee*," Cara said. "No wonder Yoder's Mercantile does so well!"

"I'm not surprised that the Yoders are expanding," observed Daniel. He reached for a chocolate-chip cookie and bit into it, talking with his mouth full. "Their store has become one of the most popular places in town among the *Englischers*, and it's only been a few years. They're smart, the Yoders."

"*Ja*, they are," agreed Cara. "They were smart to start a cannery."

"And they were even smarter to hire you," added Matthew. He winked at his future wife. "Your qualifications are what will make the cannery succeed."

"Hey, let's have a big mutual admiration party," observed Eva tartly, but with a smile. "You can all discuss how smart we are while I put this little one down for his nap." She rose, Eli fast asleep in her arms.

Matthew chuckled. "She's right. We're too *hochmut*. Daniel, tell me about the farm. Have you sown your winter wheat yet?"

With the toddler down for a nap, the adults moved into the living room with more comfortable seats. The men discussed farming while Cara and Eva exchanged views on canning and kids. The older children ran in and out of the house, sometimes leaving the door open to the chill outside air. Cara enjoyed the pleasant chaos the *kinder* added.

It wasn't until little Eli awoke with a wail that Matthew rose. "We should probably be going," he said to Cara. "Now that you know your way here, don't hesitate to drop by."

"*Ja,* for sure and certain," repeated Daniel. "I know Eva is anxious to get to know you better."

"I will," said Cara, rising to her feet. "*Danke* for having us over."

Matthew and Cara left the house and went through the yard gate to where the horse was patiently waiting under a tree.

"Ooh, that's *hübsch*!" exclaimed Cara, zooming in on some tall, button-like yellow flowers growing in the field across from the Hostetlers' house. "What are they?"

"Tansy," he replied, untying the horse. "They're a common fall flower around here. I've always liked them since they just seem to glow against the autumn landscape. Pity there aren't any in town."

She gathered a fast armful of the tall, tough stems. "I wonder if they can be planted in the backyard of the boarding-house?" she mused as she climbed into the buggy and examined the plants. "The leaves are so feathery."

"*Ja*, they'd probably grow fine. You're to consider the backyard your own," he added as he clucked to the horse. "Anything you want to plant, whether flowers or vegetables, feel free to do so."

His eyes on the road, he didn't notice she had detached a flower from its stem until she slipped it through the strap of his suspender.

"What's that for?" he asked, charmed.

She gave him the full wattage of her beautiful smile. "For everything," she replied. "You're so *gut* to me, Matthew, in every respect. *Danke* for taking me to visit your sister. I think it won't be long until she's like my sister too." She slipped an arm through his and leaned against him, watching the scenery as it passed.

Matthew swallowed hard. This affectionate side of his mail-order bride was something he liked very much. In fact, there were times full-out *love* threatened to overwhelm him. It brought out an overpowering urge to protect her.

In some respects, Cara was an extraordinarily independent woman. It took much strength of character to defy her family and travel across the entire country to build a new life with a stranger. It took even more strength and intelligence to accumulate the impressive professional experience she had, and to manage and operate a cannery single-handed. He felt blessed beyond belief she had agreed to become his wife.

Now, if only his parents would accept her as wholeheartedly as Eva did. The specter of losing his position at the boardinghouse still worried him.

"Penny for your thoughts?" she said into the silence.

He pressed her arm against his and decided on only partial honesty. "Counting my blessings," he said. "So very glad you came to the Amish settlement here. Cara, I foresee a lot of happiness in our married life, *Gott* willing."

"*Ja*, I do too." She was silent a moment, still snuggled against him, looking out at the passing landscape. "You're so different than Andrew," she added after a few moments. "There was always an undertone of... I don't know, maybe 'impatience' is the right word, when we were together. In retrospect, him dumping me was the best thing that could have happened, even if it wounded my pride at the time. I wonder what he's doing now," she ended thoughtfully.

"Did he marry?"

"He said he was going to, but now I think it was just an excuse. Either way, I wish him well." She looked up at him. "One thing is certain, you're far better-looking."

He burst out laughing. *"Danke.* It's never anything I gave much thought to, but I'm glad you approve."

The buggy approached the edge of town, and Cara withdrew her arm to permit him to maneuver the horse more easily. He missed her closeness right away.

Soon enough they approached the boardinghouse courtyard. "I'll go stable the horse," he said as he tossed some keys from his pocket to Cara. "Go ahead and let yourself in."

"Ja gut." She descended from the buggy and took her bundle of flowers and his keys, and went inside. He looked after her for a moment, admiring her tall,

slender figure, before turning his attention to the horse.

After he had the buggy put away and the animal stabled, he went indoors to find she had placed the tansy flowers in a tall canning jar on the front desk. He smiled at the feminine touch. It occurred to him that was what he'd been missing all this time—a woman's touch.

He entered his private quarters to see she had already lit a fire in the wood cookstove, warming the chill room. "Hungry?" she asked.

"*Ja*, actually I am." He divested himself of his coat and hat, hanging both on hooks near the door.

"I thought I could make a ground beef casserole. I have ground beef I canned earlier this week..." She pointed to a quart jar resting on the counter. "So it won't take much time to make."

"Anything I can do?"

"*Nein.* It's Sunday. Except for chores, neither of us should be working." She withdrew a recipe book from a shelf, flipped it open to a page and peered at the directions.

Matthew busied himself bringing in a load of firewood for the woodstove, but what he really wanted to do was just watch Cara going about her tasks. She gave off a feeling of calm efficiency, and he realized how much he enjoyed seeing her make herself at home in his home.

And later on, when he sat down at the table opposite her and dished up some of the casserole, he had a minor revelation.

The food wasn't just a meal. It was an offering of love.

No wonder it tasted so good.

He couldn't wait to marry her and eat every meal while sitting across the table from her.

Chapter Nine

Cara wiped a bead of sweat from her forehead. Though the temperature outside was chilly, the cannery was warm and steamy.

She was in full production mode this week. Matthew was working on a carpentry project with his father at the farm, so she was alone in the cannery. All three pressure canners were full—today's recipe to be sold in the Yoders' store was an onion relish—and she had four water-bath canners going as well. She was prepping the last of Miriam Lapp's garden produce to pressure-can after the batch of onion relish was complete.

To top it off, she was tired…and worried. She was starting to feel her pregnancy, and being on her feet all day was getting tougher, which was why she was grateful for the stool she could sit on while prepping vegetables. She really needed to talk to Mabel Yoder about hiring an assistant to help her.

Her worry centered around the rising urgency to confess her condition to Matthew. His affection for her was clearly growing, but not for someone carrying another man's child…

"Excuse me?"

Startled, Cara looked up. The middle-aged *Englisch* woman, Lucy Naylor, stood in the connecting doorway between the cannery and the retail store.

Cara gave her a lukewarm smile. "Good morning." She wasn't in the mood to deal with an argumentative *Englischer* who didn't believe in proper canning procedures. "May I help you?"

"Good morning." Lucy stepped farther into the cannery and came to stand before the stainless steel table where Cara was cutting vegetables. "I came to apologize."

Whatever Cara had expected, it wasn't this. She paused, knife in hand. "Apologize? For what?"

The woman looked calm but wary. "For dismissing your concerns about my canning procedures. I took your advice and looked it up, and you're right. I should not have been water-bath canning my vegetables."

A genuine smile crept across Cara's face. She laid down the knife. "What else did you learn?"

"A fair bit, actually. I basically fell down a rabbit hole, researching more and more information, and learned everything you said was right and I was wrong. So I wanted to apologize, and then ask a question."

"*Ja*, sure."

"If I were to bring my garden produce in, will you show me how to can it properly?"

"Of course!" Cara straightened up on the stool, her fatigue forgotten. Training people in correct procedures was one of her greatest professional joys. "I'd be happy to!"

"Thank you. I'd appreciate it." Lucy looked around the room. "I've only ever used a water bath, so I'm ignorant of a lot of things. Are those pressure canners?"

"*Ja.*" Cara slid off the stool and grabbed a towel to wipe her hands. "I'm canning up onion relish at the moment. The Yoders will sell it in their store when it's ready. I'm also working on preserving the harvest of a lady in our church who just had a baby and needed some help."

Lucy walked close to the massive pressure canners, eyeing them warily. "How does this work?"

Cara pointed to the gauge at the top,

as well as the stout knobs that screwed down to secure the heavy lid. "In a nutshell, pressure canning is putting jars in a steamy environment and superheating it above the temperature of boiling water. A water bath..." she pointed to the four massive covered pots bubbling on burners "...can never get above the temperature of boiling water. But in a pressure canner, temperatures can go many degrees higher, which kills off harmful bacteria such as the ones that cause botulism."

"And you don't pressure-can everything, just to be safe?"

"*Nein.* I mean, no. Only low-acid foods need to be pressure-canned. High-acid foods, which include most fruits, are safe to can in a water bath."

Encouraged by the older woman's obvious interest, Cara walked Lucy slowly through the cannery, pointing out the purpose of each piece of equipment and giving an abbreviated chemistry lesson.

Lucy paused before a sturdy multi-shelved rolling cart holding dozens of jars of preserved fruits, vegetables and meats. "This is lovely," she said with satisfaction. "There's just nothing prettier than rows of colorful jars."

"*Ja*, I feel the same!" In fact, Lucy had verbalized precisely how Cara often felt—that the final products were almost an art form.

"And meats!" Lucy pointed to some jars of canned chicken and ground beef. "I didn't know you can preserve meat."

"*Ja*, it's very straightforward. For quart jars, it's ninety minutes in the pressure canner at about fifteen pounds of pressure…"

"I have so much to learn," Lucy said thoughtfully. She gave Cara a half-mocking smile. "It seems strange to have a young woman know so much more about this than I do."

Cara smiled back, feeling a dawning friendship with the *Englischer*. "Only because I've been canning since I was five years old, and my grandmother showed me how. I worked in a commercial cannery in Pennsylvania for several years before coming out here. I have Master Food Preserver credentials on top of everything else. But don't worry, I can teach you everything you need to know."

"Should I get a pressure canner?" Lucy moved back toward the massive pieces of equipment quietly bubbling on the burners.

"*Ja*, if you're going to can up vegetables or meat at home, but you don't need one this big. The company that makes this particular canner makes them in several sizes. This is their largest. I can recommend the size of my own personal canner, which holds seven quart jars or eighteen pint jars at a time."

A kitchen timer started beeping. "Excuse me a moment," said Cara, and she scanned the pressure gauges and peeked under the lid of the water-bath canners.

Then she reset the kitchen timer and clipped it to the neckline of her apron.

"What is that for?" inquired Lucy, nodding at the timer.

"I keep timers going for every canner in production," explained Cara. "When using a pressure canner, it's necessary to make sure the pressure stays at the correct level, so I check it every few minutes to see if I need to adjust the heat. For the water-bath canners, as you no doubt know, I have to make sure they stay at a rolling boil."

"I find myself anxious to learn more," admitted Lucy. She eyed the pile of vegetables. "Do you need help?"

Cara's eyebrows shot up into her hairline. "But these vegetables aren't yours! Why would you want to help process someone else's garden produce?"

"Because I have to start somewhere, don't I? I have a couple hours to kill if you want a hand right now."

"Then *ja*, I'll gladly take you up on it."

Cara fetched a cotton apron with a loop neck. "You might want to wear this."

"Thank you." The woman lifted the loop over her head and tied the strings behind her back. Without being prompted, she went to a sink to wash her hands, which Cara took as a good sign.

Within moments, Lucy was seated on another stool on the opposite side of the stainless steel table, peeling carrots. Cara noted the woman's movements were brisk and efficient—the *Englischer* was clearly experienced with food prep. The pile of carrots waiting to be peeled decreased rapidly.

"I'll show you how to use the commercial food processor," offered Cara. She demonstrated how to feed the carrots into the machine.

"I thought the Amish didn't use electricity?" inquired Lucy.

"In our homes, *nein*. But this is a professional cannery," replied Cara. "Sometimes we must conform to legal standards when preparing or selling food products, such as proper refrigeration. If I were preparing these carrots in my own kitchen, I would simply slice them by hand. Now watch how I sterilize the jars..."

Lucy's interest was infectious. Cara found she enjoyed the *Englisch* woman's curiosity and occasional assistance. When it came time to turn the heat off under the pressure canners, Lucy listened intently as Cara explained how the pressure must slowly come to zero as part of the processing requirements for the food product. The older woman helped remove the jars of pears from the water baths, lifting the jars with confidence and resting them on racks.

"I could get to enjoy this," she said at one point, looking at the cooling jars on the racks. "I've always liked canning, but the only thing I've ever done is water-bath canning."

"Well, the onion relish is ready to come out of the canner," said Cara. "Would you like to help me prepare the carrots to put in the canner? Or do you have to get home?"

"Yes, I'd like that! And no, my husband is at work and won't be home for another few hours. I have time."

So the older woman figuratively rolled up her sleeves and assisted in filling quart jars with sliced carrots, adding pickling salt, and topping them with steaming clean water. She watched intently as Cara lowered the jars into the canners, using racks to make two levels, then secured the lids with the knobs.

"That's all there is to it?" Lucy asked.

"Pretty much, *ja*. The main thing about pressure canning is to use these kitchen timers to remind me to constantly monitor the pressure and not get distracted with something else." Cara started punching buttons on the little battery-operated timers. She placed one near each of the canners, and clipped another to her apron neck. "I check them every five minutes, from start to finish."

"Amazing." Lucy gave her a sunny smile. "May I come back tomorrow and do some more?"

"If you want to bring in your own garden produce, I'll walk you through canning it," replied Cara. "However I'll ask you to bring your own jars and lids."

"That's not a problem, I have plenty. Thank you! This has been fun."

Cara shook hands and watched as the *Englischer* disappeared through the connecting door to the Yoders' store. She wondered if the Yoders would be interested in hiring Lucy as her cannery assistant. She smiled to herself and got back to work.

Matthew grunted a bit as he moved a repaired side section of the milking stall back into place for his father.

"Danke, sohn," Eli Miller said. Once the section was upright, he expertly joined

his son in securing the stall back together. The older man picked up the thread of the conversation. "She's a lovely woman, Matthew, but you know my concerns. I don't think a mail-order bride is the way to go."

Matthew did his best to keep any trace of annoyance out of his voice. "Then how was I supposed to find a woman to marry?"

"I don't know, but…"

"Then you can't refuse me this chance," interrupted Matthew curtly. "What about Cara don't you like? I think *Mamm* was quite taken with her."

"There's nothing wrong that I see, it's just a feeling…" Eli's voice trailed off. He had a stubborn look on his face as he turned a screw.

Matthew decided to try a different approach. He kept his voice quiet. "You've been opposed from the start with me using *The Budget* to advertise, but you've never told me why. What's behind your opposition?"

Eli sighed and paused in his work. He kept his eyes on the board in front of him. "It's not a story I like to tell," he said. "But maybe it's time you know."

Matthew also paused. It wasn't like his father to keep secrets. He waited patiently.

"You remember your Uncle Micah?" Eli said. "He moved to Florida when you were pretty young, but he came back to visit us in Ohio several times."

"*Ja*, I remember him."

"Well, he advertised for a wife in *The Budget*. This would have been, oh, probably just after you were born."

"And what happened?"

"A very nice woman answered his advertisement. They courted for a bit and he was smitten. But she pushed to get married right away. Finally he found out why—she was pregnant. Micah took it hard. I think that's one of the reasons he moved so far away. To escape the humiliation."

Matthew felt stunned. He remembered his uncle as being a cheerful and jovial man. "Is that why he never got married?"

"*Ja*, I'm sure it was part of it. He could easily have married someone he met in Florida, but I think the whole situation soured him on women for life."

"But that's not what's happening here," Matthew replied, with an edge in his voice. "Cara answered my advertisement because she had been dumped by her betrothed, same as me. She also had a hard home life. The situations aren't the same."

"Maybe not, but all I'm saying is you still don't know her all that well. Take things slow."

Matthew thought about his promise to her to get married this November rather than next year. While he understood his father's need for caution, he found himself impatient to marry sooner rather

than later. He wanted a wife. He wanted
a proper home life. Was that too much
to ask?

Eli stepped back and surveyed their
handiwork. "That should do it. *Danke*,
my boy, I couldn't have done it alone."

"*Ja*, sure. No problem, *Daed*." Matthew
gave the structure a brief shake, testing
its strength, but the pieces were solid and
didn't move. "I should get back. I have a
surprise planned for Cara for lunch."

"What kind of surprise?"

"A picnic in the park."

Eli gave him a guarded smile. "Go on,
now. Go court your bride."

Matthew embraced his father and
headed out to hitch up the horse.

He had been planning this picnic for a
few days, hoping to wring some enjoy-
ment from the lingering autumn warmth.
The trees in the park were in beautiful
color, and he suspected Cara might be
missing some of the autumn shades from

Pennsylvania in this largely coniferous part of the country.

He had some delicacies he'd purchased from the Yoders' store—pastries made by Esther Mast, delicate cheeses made by Aaron Lapp, as well as water crackers—and he had assembled some sandwiches of a type he knew she liked. A colorful quilt, an old-fashioned picnic basket, and his surprise should be complete.

Despite his father's warning for caution, he found he liked courting. He liked planning surprises for Cara. He liked seeing the joy on her face whenever she saw the progress on the pantry he was building for her. He liked doing whatever it took to make her happy. He sometimes wondered about the flashes of sadness or moodiness he caught her in, but attributed it to the natural adjustment it took when moving from one community to another all the way across the country.

He pulled the buggy up to the boardinghouse. It was a few minutes before noon, when she normally took her lunch break, so he stabled and brushed the horse, then hurried inside to pack the goodies into the picnic basket. He took the already-folded quilt, grabbed the basket and headed toward Yoder's Mercantile three blocks away.

The store was busy, so he didn't bother Abe or Mabel. Instead he walked through the connecting door into the cannery and saw Cara sitting on a high wooden stool, dicing vegetables. The air was steamy, and he saw a lot of huge kettles and pots in use.

"Guten tag," he greeted her.

She looked up and smiled. *"Guten tag!* How went the project with your *daed*?"

"Fine. All finished. He sends his greetings." The last part was not quite accurate, but he hoped it would make her feel good.

"What's that you're carrying?" She eyed his burdens.

He hefted the picnic basket and the folded quilt. "I thought I'd see if I could sweet-talk you into having a picnic in the park with me. It's a beautiful day out, and the trees are in full color."

Her face crumpled. "*Ach*, I'd love to, but I have all the canners going full steam. I can't get away right now."

"Oh." Matthew had to resist the urge to clunk himself upside the head. Of course she couldn't get away at will, not when she was in the middle of projects. Why hadn't he considered that?

An alternative occurred to him. "Then how about a picnic right here?" He pointed across the room to the unfinished construction area. "I'll spread this quilt on the floor and we can pretend we're sitting on grass."

"Oh, Matthew..." She chuckled, put down her knife and slid off the stool. "That sounds like fun!"

Pleased, he handed her the picnic basket while he opened the quilt and settled it on the concrete floor.

"What inspired you to think about a picnic?" she inquired, placing the basket on the floor and folding her legs underneath her. She clipped a kitchen timer to her collar. "It's a charming idea."

"I'd been planning it for a couple of days," he admitted. "The trees in the park are looking so nice, and I figured you might be missing the autumn colors from back East. Montana has so many conifers that fall foliage is more rare." He lifted the lid of the basket and began pulling out the food.

"You went all out!" exclaimed Cara. She pointed at some of the pastries. "I recognize these from the Yoders' bakery case. Who makes them?"

"An older lady you probably met in passing after church. Her name is Esther Mast and she's an expert pastry chef. People in town love her items. The Yoders can hardly keep anything she makes in stock."

They paused for a silent blessing over the food, then Cara bit into the sandwich Matthew had made for her: salami and Swiss on rye bread.

"How long before the bakery is ready to open?" she inquired, waving her hand at the unfinished area.

"Probably not until early next year. Abe told me there's no rush, especially since I don't think they have a baker in mind yet. The one thing Abe suggested is a sort of half-wall between the bakery and the cannery, so customers don't wander over and bother you."

She chuckled. "*Gut* thinking." The timer beeped and she jumped up. "Let me check the canners." Cara went over to peer at gauges and peek under pot lids, and returned to the picnic. She reset the timer and clipped it back on her collar. "Oh, let me tell you what happened this morning!"

Matthew listened to her tale of the *Englisch* woman who came to apologize and ended up helping out for a couple hours. "I have a feeling about her," concluded Cara. "She said her kids are grown and her *hutband* works full-time. I suspect she's a bit lonely and perhaps bored. I might talk to Mabel about hiring her as an assistant. I can train her in safe and proper canning methods, and I could use the help."

Matthew hadn't given much thought to how physically hard the work was in a cannery. But he noticed Cara did seem tired. "Until that happens," he suggested, "do you want us to find a *youngie* from church who can help? She could at least peel and chop vegetables."

"*Ich weiß es nicht.* I don't know. Maybe."

He knew Cara well enough by this point to recognize her prevarication was nothing short of a cry for help. He silently vowed to talk to Mabel right away about hiring someone. For all her enthusiasm in running the cannery, he didn't want her getting burned out.

"I wonder if I could help?" he mused. "Until you get an assistant?"

"When?" she questioned. "You're working two jobs as it is. *Nein*, Matthew, that's kind of you, but I'll get by. In fact, I'm pleased by how fast things are shaping up. Just about everything I make to sell in the Yoders' store sells fast, and the canning I'm doing for church members seems to please everyone. If I'm a little tired, it's just the tiredness that comes from an honest day's work."

That was another thing he admired about Cara—she tended to look at the sunny side of things and rarely complained. Those qualities boded well for a lifelong partner.

The timer on her collar began beeping again, and she excused herself to go check the canners. He watched as she expertly monitored the gauges and status of the large pots on the stove. Under two of the pots, she turned off the heat but kept the lids on.

"Almost done with the pressure canners," she said, returning to the quilt where she seized a blueberry tart and bit into it. "These are Miriam Lapp's vegetables. I should be able to finish all her canning by this evening. Tomorrow I'm going to spend the whole day making things to sell in the store before tackling any more church projects."

"You amaze me," he said quietly, smiling into her dark eyes. "No wonder you want such a large pantry."

"It's my vocation," she said simply. "A talent *Gott* gave me."

"I look forward to finding out your other talents," he said in a flirtatious tone. "How are you at caring for babies, for example?"

She smiled, but the smile didn't quite reach her eyes. *"Gut,"* she affirmed. *"Und ja*, I suppose that's a talent I'll be using sooner rather than later."

Matthew wasn't quite sure what she meant by that, but he was far too much in love to question her.

Chapter Ten

"I've been thinking it over," Cara said as she and Matthew walked back to the boardinghouse the next afternoon. "You need to teach me the ropes of running your business. After all, it will be a part of my life too."

"There's no need," began Matthew. "You already have so much on your plate…"

"But I want to," she interrupted. "I doubt I'll ever be in a position to take it over full-time, but I need to know how to check people in if you're busy or away, and all the other duties you normally do."

"Well, if you're sure…"

"I'm sure." She resisted the urge to rest her hand on her midsection. She had loosened her apron just a bit more, and didn't think her condition was noticeable to the undiscerning eye. "Since I'm spending every day at the cannery, I don't know your day-to-day schedule except when you're working on the bakery area."

"You know, I actually do have a guest checking in later this evening," he replied. "I can give you a fast tutorial on the check-in procedure and then stand by while you do it yourself, if you like."

She chuckled. "A trial by fire?"

"Something like that." He smiled. "Ninety-nine percent of my guests are wonderful. I'm sure the man checking in tonight will be in that category."

"So what's the one percent like? What are some of the issues you'd had to deal with?"

"Hmm. I've had some guests who are simply noisy—playing music, mostly. A few times I've had to deal with something broken. Several people have simply trashed the room on purpose. I had one couple get into a loud fight—I actually had to summon the police over that one."

She stared at him with wide eyes. "You're kidding!"

"It's not the way it usually is!" he added hurriedly. "You've been here several weeks now—have any of the guests ever disturbed you?"

"*Nein,* not at all. Sometimes I'm not even aware they're in the building."

"Exactly."

"So what happens to the difficult guests? Do you kick them out?"

"If they're just being noisy, I simply ask them to keep it down and most of them comply. The couple that was fighting, I kicked out. The ones who trashed the room, I charged them for damages and put them on a blacklist."

"Oh, so you can keep people from checking in again if they've caused problems before?"

"*Ja*, of course. That's one of the things I'll show you—my blacklist."

They approached the boardinghouse and entered through the courtyard door. The building was quiet, but Cara knew two of the rooms were occupied—though the guests were likely not in at the moment.

"Let me unlock the back," said Matthew. "That way we can leave our hats and coats." They walked behind the front desk, and he unlocked the door to his private quarters and left it open. They divested themselves of their outerwear, then he returned to the front desk.

"This is the reservation book," he said, drawing out an oversize spiral notebook with colorful tabs. He flipped it open to the front pages, where the layout of each floor was illustrated and kept in a plastic sleeve. She bent over the illustration, examining it. "You can see how each room has the floor number built into it, such as Room 204 or 101. The first floor has four guest rooms, and depending on how large our family gets, I'm in a position to enclose those into private quarters." He grinned at her.

Cara felt herself blush. "*Gut* idea," she murmured.

"But unless we're completely booked, I prefer to check guests into the second or third floor rooms, and reserve the ground floor in case we have guests with a disability. The ground-floor rooms are wheelchair accessible."

"I see."

"The second and third floors have six rooms each. I gave you the nicest room since it has a tree shading it during the hottest part of summer. Each room has a private bath. I opted not to include a television set in any of the rooms since no one expects that in an Amish boarding-house. Each room has a propane heater for colder weather."

She chuckled. "Do the *Englischers* ever complain about no television?"

"A couple of times, *ja*. But I make it clear from the beginning, so most are fine with it. Now this..." He flipped open the notebook to a red tab. "These are the reservations for October. As you can see, as each room gets reserved, I write down the full contact information for the guest, including times they anticipate checking in. I always use pencil, because often reservations change. But this layout lets me see at a glance which rooms are available. Most of our guests aren't here overnight, but for a few days at a time. Sometimes they stay longer—weeks or even months. I give a discount for longer stays."

"Who would stay for such a long time?"

"Mostly field workers—traveling nurses, forestry personnel, that kind of thing."

"Do you clean the rooms every day?"

"*Nein.* This is a boardinghouse, not a hotel. I'll make clean towels available, and for longer-staying guests I'll change the sheets once a week, but the rooms only get completely cleaned between guests."

"I see. Maybe you should give me a routine chore, something I can do every day, to make me feel like I'm contributing something."

"But you already work so hard at the cannery," he began.

She waved a hand. "So do you. Truly, Matthew, I want to feel more vested in this business, especially if it's going to be *our* business. What would you like me to do every day?"

He rubbed his chin. "Perhaps folding laundry? Let me show you." He led her through a closed door into a large side room.

The room was strung with clotheslines, some with sheets drying, and featured numerous sturdy drying racks with towels. A large table had a neat stack of towels on one end. Two washing machines stood in a corner.

"These are Amish-made propane washing machines," he said, pointing to the machines. "I dry all the linens by rack or line. If you'd like to take over folding sheets and towels, I'd be grateful."

"*Ja*, sure! I'd be happy to." It was an easy task, and one she was happy to do. "Where should I put them when they're folded?"

"Here." He showed her a wall unit of large cubicles, each with a room number on it. "Some of the rooms have twin beds, some have full, and some have king-size. Each sheet is tagged what room it goes to. Towels go here…" He showed her some wide shelves. "They don't have specific room assignments. But *ja*, folding linens would be a big help."

Cara looked around at the facility. It was a blend of Plain and modern solutions common among Amish businesses that catered to the public. She had seen such mixtures often enough in Pennsylvania. It pleased her to have such a useful facility for her own use. "I think I'm going to be very happy living here," she murmured.

Matthew heard her and a pleased smile spread across his face. "I'm glad to hear that," he said.

She locked eyes with him for a moment, and she saw longing in their depths. She felt a return tug within her, and—confused—dropped her gaze to the floor.

Matthew led the way out of the laundry room to the front desk. "I forgot—here is the receipt book. All customers get a copy of their stay information, and I keep a copy here." He showed her a file.

She glanced through it. "Do you do your own accounting?"

"*Nein.* You know Thomas Kemp, the Yoders' bookkeeper? He has his own business, so he keeps my books too." He smiled. "In fact, I was delighted to give it to him. He's a natural at juggling numbers, but it's a struggle for me, so he keeps track of everything."

"I like Thomas. Miriam is his sister, *ja*?"

"*Ja.* Oh, by the way, Miriam and Aaron have invited us over tomorrow afternoon. Aaron wants to show me something new he was tinkering with in his shop, and I think Miriam said she had a recipe she wanted you to try, perhaps one you could can up and carry in the Yoders' store. Just a short visit since they have something they're doing in the evening."

"That will be nice. I like Miriam." She gestured toward the desk. "What are some of your other duties?"

"A lot of it is keeping things clean. Sweeping, dusting, laundry, that kind of thing. Also, it's helpful to have a list of amenities in the town and surrounding areas for people who want to do touristy things." He pulled another notebook from under the desk and opened it, flipping through pages. "These are the attractions in the area, as well as a lot of business cards from businesses around town in case someone has need of a hardware item or birthday present." He flipped to another page in the notebook. "I also keep a list of all the churches in the area for those who are interested."

"I'm impressed." Matthew's system was simple but effective. It denoted a man who was efficient and organized. "So let's say your guest walked through the door right now. How would you check him in?"

He showed her the routine he followed, beginning with confirming the information in the reservation book and ending with providing the guest with a key. "I have multiple keys for each room," he explained, showing her the key storage cabinet. "It's not uncommon for guests to unthinkingly walk away with a key when they leave."

"Okay, I think I can do this." She smiled at him. "As you suggested, let me check in the guest when he arrives, with you hovering at my elbow to make sure I don't mess up."

"Ja gut." His eyes were warm with affection as he looked at her. "Meanwhile, what do you say to some dinner? I'm hungry."

"Omelet?" she suggested.

"Ja, with some sausages and hash browns. *Komm,* we'll make breakfast for dinner." He offered her the crook of his elbow, and she slipped her hand through it, feeling a surge of affection for this kind man as she walked with him into the private quarters of the boardinghouse.

Matthew was beyond pleased to hear Cara was interested in learning the inner workings of the boardinghouse, though privately he doubted she would ever have much of an opportunity to be very hands-on. But she was right: if she was going to live here, she needed to know the basics in case he was absent or called away.

"Did Mabel say anything more about hiring an assistant for you in the cannery?" he asked with a mouthful of omelet.

"Actually, *ja*." Cara wiped her mouth with a napkin. "I recommended Lucy Naylor. She came back this week with her own garden produce, and I walked her through proper canning procedures for the vegetables. It's funny—it's like a whole new world opened up to her. I could almost see the dawning wonder on her face as we removed the processed jars from the pressure canners. She is all enthusiasm. Mabel came in at one point and we all chatted a bit. After Lucy left, I mentioned the possibility to Mabel about hiring Lucy as an assistant. Mabel said she would have to talk it over with Abe, but otherwise seemed open to it." She took a bite of sausage in her omelet. "Of course I have no idea if Lucy will even be interested, but I get the impression she might—"

She broke off as Matthew heard a small bell ring from the front desk.

"That must be our new guest," he said, rising. "Ready to check him in?"

"*Ja.*" She placed her napkin on the table, stood up and smoothed down her apron.

Matthew followed her as she made her way to the front desk, where a middle-aged man with thick glasses stood waiting.

"Good evening," Cara said with a smile. "You must be Mr. Rodriguez."

"Yes," he replied. He extracted a credit card from his wallet. "I hope I'm not checking in too late?"

"*Nein,* not at all." With admirable confidence, Cara took the man's card, fitted a credit card slip into the manual imprinter. She paused as she realized the card had no raised numbers, so she seized a pen and began filling out the slip by hand.

"Is this filled in correctly?" she inquired of Matthew, showing him the paper.

"New at the job?" inquired Mr. Rodriguez with a smile.

"*Ja*, first day," she replied.

Matthew scanned the paper and handed it back to Cara. "Be sure to write down his phone number here," he indicated. "Otherwise it's fine."

Cara duly wrote down the man's number, and he signed the slip.

"Do you have a preference for what floor you want?" she inquired. "The first floor is most convenient, especially for those with mobility issues, but the third floor has the best view."

"Hmm. I'd be willing to try the third floor," he said.

Cara turned to Matthew. "Which room do you recommend?"

"Room 3C," he replied. He nodded toward the key cabinet and handed her the master key, but made no move to fetch the key himself. Instead he said to the man,

"The room is heated with a propane wall heater. Full instructions for turning it on are over the heater, but if it gives you trouble, don't hesitate to let me know."

Cara opened the door of the cabinet, found the proper key and handed it to the man. "Do you need help with your luggage?"

"No, thank you. I appreciate the help." With a smile, the man took the key, picked up his suitcase and headed up the stairs.

Matthew waited until his guest was out of earshot before smiling at Cara. "Nicely done."

"Danke." She chuckled. "It was kind of fun, almost like playacting." She stopped smiling and suddenly looked concerned. "I forgot to ask him how long he'll be staying."

"It says here." Matthew showed her the place in the reservation book. "Four nights. Oh, and since he's the only guest at the moment, he could have his choice of room, but that won't be an option during times we're booked up."

"What happens when you're fully booked and someone wants a room?"

"It's happened a few times, usually during the holidays or when the local high school has its graduation. If we're busy, I refer people to Simon Troyer's B and B outside of town, or there're a few places in town that informally rent rooms. Assuming the town's two motels are booked, that is."

"Is that all we need to do right now?"

"*Ja*, except for being 'on call' when we're in the building. If I'm away, I put this up." He dragged a small sign from below the desk and set it upright. It read "Away from Desk. Will be Back Soon" —with a plastic clock face on which the hands could be adjusted.

Cara examined the sign. "Have you ever had anyone cause trouble when you're not here?"

"Not so far, *nein*. If there's no one here

and I'm away, I put a sign on the front door and lock the building. Speaking of which, when the desk is unattended, be sure to lock the key cabinet." He handed her his master key.

She duly locked the cabinet, then followed Matthew back into the private quarters to their unfinished meals.

Cara tasted the food, made a face and promptly slid everything into a pan and put it on the stove. "Let's let it heat up a few minutes," she said. She idly glanced around the furnished quarters with its unfinished pantry. "How old is this building, anyway?"

"At least a hundred years old." Matthew poured himself a glass of milk and sipped it. "It was in rough shape when my parents bought it, but they could see right away the structure was sound. Also, it was ideally suited for a Plain establishment since it hadn't been modernized. By law they were required to conform to electrical and plumbing standards, but had a lot of leeway to make it Plain as well."

"So your parents bought it and did all this work, but didn't want to run it as a boardinghouse?" Cara remarked, flipping the food in the pan.

"My *bruder* Mark and I both worked on it," he replied, and smiled at the memory. "Eva's *hutband*, Daniel, helped at times too. It was a fun project for us all to be involved in, and we've all taken turns running it—except for Daniel, that is— and what was nice is how supportive the townspeople were. Often times we had people just stop in to introduce them- selves and see our progress. Almost ev- eryone expressed gratitude that we were rescuing this venerable building. It was quite the goodwill project," he concluded.

"Are the people in town glad about the Amish community's businesses? The boardinghouse, the B and B, Yoder's Mercantile, and now the cannery?"

"*Ja*, very much so," he agreed. "That's

why the town's mayor first went to talk to Bishop Beiler about putting on the demonstration during the town's Mountain Days celebration. Most people who live here had never met any Amish before, and they're fascinated. Enough to make sure any new businesses are thriving as a result. It's why I think the cannery and now the bakery will be a success. But in some ways it's nicer than back in Ohio, or I imagine Pennsylvania, because we don't get buses of tourists here to watch us like zoo animals."

Cara spooned the reheated foods back to their plates, and seated herself. "I certainly won't mind living in town for a few years."

Matthew felt a wave of affection and gratitude wash over him as he took a bite of potatoes. "I like how practical you are," he said. "I know I tried to portray myself with perfect honesty in my advertisement and in our early letters, and I can't tell you how grateful I am you're willing to roll with the punches as we start our married life."

She looked at her plate. "There's so much I like out here, as opposed to back in Pennsylvania. A lot has to do with being away from my *daed*, as you can imagine, but it's more than that." She met his eyes. "I'm going to be the best wife that I possibly can, Matthew. I hope you'll never regret your choice."

Matthew had no doubts she would be a good wife for him, but this wasn't the first time she had voiced her promise along those lines. For some reason it triggered an uneasiness in him, but he couldn't pinpoint why. He decided to ask. "Why wouldn't you be? You've been just as honest and up-front with me as I have with you."

She dropped her eyes once again to her plate. "I've tried to be," she murmured, low. "But as with anyone, it will take time to learn everything about each other." She took a final bite of her food and pushed the empty plate away. "I'll go wash up."

"We'll both wash up." Matthew finished the last of the food on his plate and stood up.

While the uneasiness of that moment lingered, it was lost in the simple pleasure of tidying the kitchen with his future wife.

When at last the room was neat, she stood on tiptoe, kissed his cheek and said good-night.

Matthew watched her slim figure as she disappeared through the door into the lobby, and he dimly heard her footsteps as she ascended the stairs to her lonely room.

Then he returned to his own lonely quarters.

Chapter Eleven

"You want to hire me?" Lucy Naylor pressed a hand to her chest, her eyes wide.

"*Ja.*" Cara smiled at the older woman. It was Friday, and Cara wanted to spring the news so Lucy could think about it over the weekend. "My bosses, Abe and Mabel Yoder, have been talking about hiring an assistant for me. They were thinking about looking for someone within our church group, but frankly I'd rather have you."

"Not that I'm arguing, but why?"

Cara resumed cranking the food strainer, putting out strained tomatoes that she would cook down into sauce and paste. "Several reasons. First, you're enthusiastic. Even though you're older than me, you remind me of how excited I was when I first learned about canning. Enthusiasm goes a long way."

Lucy laughed. "I've water-bath canned for years, as you know, but never realized I was doing it wrong. Learning the proper way to do things has been eye-opening, and I can't wait to learn more."

"And that's the second reason. I can teach you correct procedures. You're a clean slate, so to speak. Since I'm producing foods that are being sold to the public, it's critical to follow FDA-approved canning methods."

"Yes, I know that now." Lucy resumed chopping bell peppers. "It almost frightens me to think how many years I was doing the wrong thing."

"And third," Cara concluded, "is that you're available. You live in town. Among our church members, *youngies*—that is, teenagers—are usually working on their farms. Besides, *youngies* may not be as dependable as I'd like. Young married women aren't available because they're too busy raising children. And older women who might otherwise be available have a long trip into town, which could get dicey in winter conditions. So, what is your answer?" Cara asked, smiling.

"Absolutely!" Lucy grinned back. "At home, I've been chattering up a storm to my husband about what I'm doing here every evening. He'll be thrilled at this offer. I've been rattling around the house since I retired, so he'll be happy I have something to do."

"I talked to Mabel yesterday, and she said she can bring you on for as many hours as you want to work." Cara named Mabel's hourly pay. "It's also variable. This isn't necessarily a nine-to-five job, I just work until I'm done. Obviously some periods will be busier, such as harvest season, and some times of the year will be much slower. This way if you need time off or have an obligation or appointment, it's not a problem."

"What an answer to prayer," murmured Lucy, her eyes on the chopping board.

Cara was surprised. It was the first reference to religion she had heard from Lucy. "Are you a woman of faith?" she inquired delicately.

"Of course. And to be honest, I've always had an interest in the Plain people," replied Lucy. "It's been fascinating watching an Amish community move into town. You'll have to forgive me if I pepper you with questions about your church. It's just a matter of curiosity, not rudeness."

"Since you're not shoving a camera in my face, I'm happy to answer any questions you have."

Cara's instincts about Lucy seemed correct. The woman was cheerful and eager, and it helped Cara immeasurably to share the workload.

Matthew walked in through the connecting door to the Yoders' store. *"Guten tag, liebling,"* he said. "Hello, Lucy."

Cara's heart gave a small jump at the sight of him, which she considered a good sign. She always looked forward to seeing him.

Rather than going straight to the other side of the room to resume work, however, Matthew paused by the stainless steel table where she and Lucy were working. "The Yoders gave me a budget to purchase a carpet and some comfortable chairs for the store," he told her. "They want to put them in here." He gestured toward the newly installed woodstove on its brick platform. "They said it might be nice for you to have a place to sit and relax for a few minutes when the canners are going but you're not working on a batch."

"Ach, that would be nice!" she exclaimed. "There's nothing to sit on here except these high stools."

"They said you should choose them because you're the one who's going to have to sit on them," he continued.

"And they trust my taste?" she quipped. "I don't have any experience in choosing such things."

"There's a furniture store three blocks down. I'm sure their salespeople can help."

"Then *ja*, sure, I'd be happy to. When do you want to go?"

"This afternoon, if you can."

She nodded. "What I have in the canners now will be finished by then, and I won't start anything new."

"Ja gut." Matthew walked to the other end of the room and donned his tool belt.

"Speaking of which…" Cara checked the kitchen timer clipped to her apron collar, slid off her high stool and went to check the pressure gauges on the canners. Then she returned to feed more tomatoes into the strainer.

"Is it true what I've heard?" Lucy asked

in a low voice, glancing over at Matthew who was too far away to hear her voice. "Is it true you're a mail-order bride?"

"*Ja*, it's true. Matthew put an advertisement in an Amish newspaper seeking a wife, and I wanted to get away from my parents, so here I am."

"That's so sweet! Like something right out of a romance novel."

Cara kept any hint of dismay from her expression. "It was a big chance, I knew," she prevaricated, "but Matthew turned out to be so much better than I'd hoped. *Gott ist gut.*"

"He *does* seem like a nice man."

"One of the nicest I've ever met. Much nicer than the one who dumped me." Lucy had already heard about Andrew. "We're still deciding whether to get married this November, or next November."

"Is there something special about November?"

"It's the traditional month for Amish weddings," she explained. "After the harvest and just before the slower winter months."

"I see." Lucy scooped the chopped bell peppers into a bowl and plucked another one from a basket. "My husband and I got married in May."

"How long have you been married?"

"Thirty-three years." Lucy's eyes took on a soft glow. "Thirty-three years, and I still love the big galoot to pieces."

"Now, *that* sounds like something from a romance novel," teased Cara. "How did you meet?"

"I like to say we met in a cemetery, just to shock people." Lucy smiled. "But it's true, though. The town where I used to live had purchased a huge plot of land for a cemetery. But because only a portion had been used for burials, they maintained the rest as a park. I would go there in the evenings to run my dog. Scott had a dog, too. That's how we met."

"And you said you have two *kinner*—two children?"

"Yes, two daughters. One is married and lives in Billings. No grandchildren yet," she added. "The other daughter is unmarried and lives in Boise."

"So this might be a pleasant way for you to get out of the house," suggested Cara.

"Yes, it's true. I've done volunteer work, but with this..." Lucy held aloft her knife. "It's like I've rediscovered a passion. I've always liked cooking, and working in a cannery combines the best of both worlds, cooking and canning."

"Mabel Yoder purchases baked goods from a lady in our church who is a pastry expert," remarked Cara. "But with an in-house bakery, they're going to have to find one or two people who are bakers. Bread sold very well at their old store back in Ohio. I'm glad they opened a cannery first, though."

"Plus they need to make sure things are done according to the proper standards," added Lucy. "The Yoders sound like smart businesspeople."

"*Ach*, they are!" exclaimed Cara. "I'm blessed they hired me to oversee the cannery."

"But one thing occurs to me…" Lucy paused in her chopping. "After you and Matthew are married, won't it be too hard to run the cannery when babies come?"

Cara nearly died inside, but she kept her face impassive as she continued feeding tomatoes into the strainer. "To use an *Englisch* expression, I'll cross that bridge when I come to it," she replied.

In fact, she had been thinking about that very issue more and more, since it was going to come sooner than anyone anticipated.

She looked at Lucy with new eyes. Could the older woman be trained to run the cannery by herself, with Cara overseeing from a distance? It was something to consider.

In fact, hiring Lucy might be the answer to prayer. Cara vowed to get Lucy's skills up to par as quickly as possible in case the older woman found herself working solo after Cara's baby was born. It was a lot to ask of a new hire, but Cara didn't have many options.

To that end, she nodded at the pile of chopped bell peppers Lucy had been working on. "Now let's see what you remember. You'll be adding those bell peppers, along with some onions and spices, to the tomatoes I'm straining to make spaghetti sauce. Should it be water-bath canned or pressure-canned?"

"Pressure-canned," Lucy answered promptly.

"Why?"

"Because the bell peppers and onions are low-acid. The rule of thumb you taught me is to process the food in accordance with the ingredient requiring the longest processing time, so I'll look up how long it takes to process bell peppers, and how long it takes to process onions, and that's how long the spaghetti sauce will be in the pressure canner."

Cara smiled. "You're going to work out just fine, Lucy."

From across the room, Matthew listened to the conversation between the women and smiled to himself. It seemed Cara had a solid friend in Lucy.

He donned kneepads and got down on his knees to start laying the vinyl flooring over the concrete. The color, selected by the Yoders, looked sufficiently like wood to fool most people, and he knew it would transform the appearance of the area. Matthew had used the material before when renovating the boardinghouse, and was familiar with its installation.

"Oh, wow." He looked up to see Cara had walked over, Lucy in her wake, to look at his progress. She had a kitchen timer clipped to her apron collar. "Matthew, it looks *wunnerschee.*"

"*Danke.* After this, I'll start constructing the bakery infrastructure, though a lot of the space will be stainless steel things like tables and rolling racks, similar to what you have in the cannery. The Yoders will choose the equipment such as the ovens and mixers. All I need to do is make sure the room is ready to receive them. I think that's why Abe authorized the purchase of an area rug and chairs, since all the messy work such as sanding and painting is already done."

"How soon before this will be open to the public?" inquired Lucy.

"Probably not until after Christmas," he replied. "They still haven't hired a baker, but when they do, this facility will be ready."

The timer on Cara's collar started beeping. She pressed the button to turn it off, then she and Lucy returned to the cannery to do whatever they needed to do. Matthew followed Cara with his eyes, admiring her from behind.

Then he returned his attention to the

flooring. There was no question it finished the look of the space. He had completed installing drywall and texturing last week, and applied the cream-colored paint a few days ago. And now, with the flooring, it was all coming together. Matthew smiled with satisfaction of a job well done.

He got about halfway across the room, laying the flooring, before his knees got tired, and he decided it would be a good time for an excursion to the furniture store.

He stood up and removed the kneepads. He looked over and saw Cara and Lucy finishing up cleaning the cannery equipment.

Cara glanced at him. "Time to go?"

"*Ja*, if it works for you."

She nodded and spoke to Lucy. "We can close down the cannery for the afternoon. You might want to talk to Thomas Kemp—he's the Yoders' bookkeeper—

about getting on payroll and filling in the proper forms."

"Thanks, I will." Lucy leaned in and gave Cara a quick hug. "I'm so excited to be working here. Thank you!"

Matthew waited until the older woman had disappeared through the connecting door into the store before wandering over. "Sounds like this will be a *gut* working relationship."

"*Ja*, I agree. She reminds me how I felt when I first learned proper canning techniques from my *grossmammi*. It feels *gut* to pass that knowledge on."

"Someday you'll pass it on to our children," he ventured to say, and gave her a warm smile.

She smiled back, her dark eyes crinkling. "What a nice thought," she said softly.

Their eyes locked for a moment or two longer before Matthew managed to break away. "*Ja*. Well. Let me get my hat."

Cara snatched her cloak from its peg by

the connecting door and tossed it around her shoulders. She locked the door behind her as she and Matthew nodded to the Yoders and stepped out into the street.

"What a beautiful afternoon." She looked around at the bright sunshine and colorful leaves along the town's Main Street.

"I thought I could take you to dinner after we make the selections at the furniture store. There's a nice little restaurant over there." He pointed.

"*Danke!* I would like that. I seldom eat out." Unprompted, she slipped her hand through the crook of his arm, sending a jolt of gladness through him.

"Don't forget, we're visiting the Lapps tomorrow," he reminded her. "Miriam thinks she has a recipe that might work for you to can up and sell in the store."

"And I have her vegetables ready to return. We can bring them with us when we visit."

The furniture store was only a couple

blocks down. Matthew had never been inside, but through the shop windows it looked like it carried a handsome selection. He opened the front door and let Cara precede him through.

"Good afternoon. May I help you?" asked a nicely dressed young woman. Her eyes flicked up to Cara's *kapp* and down her cloak, and her smile widened. She sported a name tag that read Barbara.

"Ja," said Matthew. "I'm working for Yoder's Mercantile down the street. They sent us here to choose a carpet and some comfortable chairs for a seating area associated with the new cannery and bakery area."

"Oh, the cannery! Yes, I've heard about that," said Barbara. "And I heard rumors a bakery would be opening too."

"That's the part I'm working on," said Matthew. "My name is Matthew Miller, and this is my fiancée, Cara Lengacher. She manages the cannery."

"How do you do." Barbara shook hands

with both. "We can start by looking over our selection of carpets, and if you don't find anything to your taste, we have a wide range to order from."

Matthew and Cara followed the woman to the back wall of the store, passing many handsome displays of bedroom, living room and dining room furniture.

"Here we go." Barbara stopped before a large display of area rugs. "What size are you looking for?"

"What's the largest size area rug available?"

"I'd say ten by fourteen feet," replied Barbara. "But we don't carry them that large. It would have to be ordered."

"Then *ja*, let's get that size."

"Let me show you what we have available."

Matthew and Cara began looking over the selection. "Any ideas about color?" he asked Cara, a little overwhelmed by the options.

"Well, you know I'm partial to earth tones," she replied.

"Earth tones are a good choice for a public area," agreed Barbara. "And darker colors are less likely to show dirt and stains as quickly."

"Greens and browns?" asked Cara with a glint in her eye.

He smiled. "*Ja*, greens and browns. Those are our favorite colors," he added for the salesperson.

"You might like to look through our online catalogs," invited Barbara. "That way you can sort by size, color and style."

Matthew found himself seated next to Cara in front of a computer screen, while Barbara hovered nearby, guiding them on how to search the various options. They scrolled through until they found a carpet in the correct size that fit both their tastes. "We'll take this one," he told the saleswoman.

"Yes." She noted the information. "I can order it and have it in…" she peered at the screen "…three weeks or so. Will that work?"

"*Ja*, I think so, especially since the bakery isn't open to the public yet. Now, chairs. The Yoders suggested something padded and comfortable."

"Let's walk through our showroom and you can see if any styles match what you're looking for."

It didn't take long to select several lovely and snug wingback chairs with a stylish tapestry design that complemented the carpet. Seating herself in one, Cara joked, "It's almost comfortable enough to sleep on!"

"Then it will be nice for anyone visiting the store area, or waiting for their canning project to complete." Matthew smiled at his future wife.

He made arrangements for the Yoders to pay for the selections, thanked Barbara for her assistance, and then he and Cara left the furniture store.

"That was fun," she remarked. "But I'm

glad I'm not paying for it. I had no idea furniture was so expensive."

"I had to purchase some when furnishing the boardinghouse," he replied. "But most of it was ordered from Amish companies back East. That was expensive enough." He re-tucked her hand through the crook of his arm as they crossed the street toward the restaurant. "But you're right, I'm glad that wasn't my money we were spending."

The Cooking Pot restaurant had a cozy feel. It was too early for the dinner rush and there weren't many customers.

Cara removed her cloak and draped it over the back of the dining chair. "It's getting cooler," she remarked. "I can sense the change of seasons."

"Winters here are nice," he replied. "Not as bitterly cold as some of the cold snaps we'd get in Ohio, I think in part because we don't have as much humidity. We can get a fair bit of snow, though..."

He trailed off as the waitress approached with glasses of water. Matthew nodded for Cara to make her selection, then he did the same. After the waitress left, Matthew continued his thoughts. "The one thing I don't like about winter, though, is I am mostly alone in the boardinghouse. I mean, of course there are often guests in the building, but I'm mostly alone in my quarters. Even though we're not married yet, I'm very glad to be able to share those lonely winter evenings with you. Maybe I can make you a special table for jigsaw puzzles," he added.

"I'd like that!" Cara smiled at him, her dark eyes glowing. "It's not exactly that I dreaded winter back home, but more like I dreaded being in the same house as my *daed* with fewer opportunities to get out. In some ways it will be nice to spend the winter in town too, rather than farther out in the settlement."

"*Ja,* the townspeople decorate very nicely for the holidays," agreed Matthew. "I like this town. Since it's the county seat, and widely isolated from any nearby metropolis, it has just about anything we need within a mile or so."

Matthew held up his glass of water and waited until she did the same. Then he said, "I propose a toast. To the most perfect woman I know."

Cara clinked glasses with him, but he noticed she hesitated for the briefest instant. "No one is perfect, Matthew," she said, and it seemed her smile was strained. "But I hope I can live up to your expectations."

Chapter Twelve

That night, Cara slept badly, tossing and turning till dawn. Lately, Matthew had been making more and more statements reflecting his utter devotion to her future happiness. It was heartrending in light of the secret child she carried. She knew the time was coming when she must tell him the truth. "Please, *Gott*," she prayed. "Don't let him turn me out when he hears."

If he *did* choose to turn her out, she would be wise to make contingency plans. She cupped her belly protectively, feeling the slight swell of unborn child.

Should she give the baby up for adoption? As painful as that was, it might be the best choice. Gifting the child to a childless couple would allow her to move on and rebuild her life elsewhere. But who could help her with that process?

The answer rose in her mind: Miriam Lapp. Of course. She was a midwife. And since she and Matthew were visiting that afternoon, Cara would delicately probe the extent of Miriam's knowledge about such a process.

If Matthew should turn her out of the boardinghouse after learning of her deception, then Miriam might know someone who would be willing to take her in. Or perhaps she could cobble together a place to stay in the cannery? It was a desperate thought, but she was starting to get into a desperate mindset.

She dragged herself out of bed and went into the bathroom to splash her face and lament over the dark circles under her eyes. It couldn't be helped. Any evidence of fatigue could be hidden under a bright smile anyway.

Unfortunately, she dreaded being with Matthew all day without a specific task in mind to distract her. Even though it was a Saturday, she decided to spend a couple hours in the cannery finishing up a project.

"But it's Saturday!" protested Matthew when she informed him of her intent over morning tea.

"*Ja*, I know. But if I finish up this one task today, it will give me a jumpstart on Monday. I'll be back in plenty of time to get ready to visit Miriam and Aaron."

"Well, if you're sure…"

She smiled at him. "I'm sure. In fact, since I have Miriam's garden produce canned up, why don't you swing by the cannery in the buggy and we can load them? I'll make sure they're boxed and ready for travel."

"*Ja gut.*"

So after breakfast, Cara walked to the

Yoders' store and disappeared into the cannery to work for several hours. She made sure Miriam's ten dozen quart jars of garden produce were packed and ready by the time Matthew pulled up at two o'clock.

"I'm sure Miriam is relieved you were able to help her out," remarked Matthew as he directed the horse out of town, boxes of full canning jars carefully stacked in back.

"*Ja*, it all worked out as far as timing. Her baby arrives just as the garden is ready to harvest, and I arrive just in time to can it up for her."

Miriam and Aaron's home was a charming little log cabin set well back from the road. A huge black Newfoundland dog rose from the porch as they pulled up, wagging his tail in greeting.

"That's Major," said Matthew, nodding at the dog as he set the buggy's brake. "He's friendly."

"He's beautiful." Cara climbed down from the buggy and patted the dog.

"*Guten tag*, Cara, Matthew," greeted Aaron from the porch.

"*Guten tag,*" she returned, smiling. Despite his heavily scarred face, Aaron had an expression of utter peace and contentment about him. To her surprise, she found herself envying him that quality. It had been a long time since she'd known such peace.

"Miriam's waiting for you inside," Aaron told her. "But I have to warn you, she made some sort of mistake in the kitchen and it's a bit smoky in the house."

"We brought all her canning," said Matthew. He reached into the back of the buggy and picked up a box containing a dozen quart jars. "Let's get these unloaded first."

Miriam emerged onto the porch, holding her tiny infant. "Let me put the baby down and I'll help," she offered.

"*Nein*, we've got it," said Matthew.

"Shall we just put them on the kitchen table?"

"Ja, bitte." Miriam stepped aside to allow passage through the door.

The moment Cara stepped inside, she smelled a strong hot-pepper scent, almost enough to make her eyes water. As Aaron had warned, the air was a touch smoky. She coughed. "Peppers?" she asked Miriam.

"Ja, I was trying a chutney recipe," the new mother replied, "and it called for pan-frying some chilies in oil at very hot temperatures. I got distracted while changing the baby and didn't realize how thick the pepper fumes got. I wanted to have you taste-test the chutney and see if it's a recipe you'd be interested in using in the cannery. *Ach, danke!"* she exclaimed as the men deposited boxes of quart jars on the table.

Despite some open windows, both men started coughing from the acrid air. "Matthew, let's get out of here," offered Aaron. They disappeared into Aaron's workshop.

"Would you like some tea?" inquired Miriam.

"*Ja, bitte.* I'll hold the *boppli*," Cara offered eagerly.

"*Danke.* He's sleepy at the moment." Miriam handed off her son. "I was hoping he'd nap for a bit before we leave. We're going to go look at a milk cow for sale in about an hour," she added.

Cara sat down on a kitchen chair, cradling the tiny infant. Her arms thrilled with the sensation of holding the baby. "I'm surprised his eyes aren't watering with the pepper fumes," she teased.

"*Ja*, it turned out a bit stronger than I anticipated." Miriam coughed into her apron. "I'm going to open one more window to see if it helps." She slid open the window over the sink. "Apparently panfrying chilies isn't the right way to go for this recipe. Things got a bit out of control." She poured tea and sat down opposite Cara. "Would you like me to take him back?" she inquired, nodding at the baby.

"Nein." Cara cuddled the baby closer. "It's such a pleasure to hold an infant, and I imagine your arms could use a break."

"A bit, *ja*." Miriam sipped her tea, then put her mug down on the table with a small thump. There was a moment's silence, then Miriam asked quietly, "When are you due?"

Cara gasped, feeling the blood drain from her face. She stared at Miriam, who watched her with compassionate eyes. "How did you know?" she whispered.

Miriam shrugged. "I'm not just a midwife—I'm a certified nurse-midwife, a registered nurse and an emergency medical technician. I can recognize the signs. I'm guessing you're, what, four and a half months along?"

Cara felt tears start to her eyes. *"J-ja,"* she stuttered.

"You're going to have to tell Matthew before the wedding, you know."

"I plan to." Cara knew her words sounded defensive. "I have no intention of trapping him into thinking the baby is his. I'll be too far along for that anyway. But I had to get to *know* him first."

"What happened? How did you become pregnant?"

Cara stared at the infant in her arms, wondering if her own baby would look this beautiful. Andrew had been a handsome man, so it was likely. The silence in the kitchen was broken only by the ticking of a clock.

"My…my… I was being courted by a man named Andrew," she began at last. "He was pushier than he should have been about—about getting intimate before the wedding. I gave in, once, and apparently that's all it took. A few days later, shortly before the wedding, he dumped me and suddenly announced he was courting someone else. I don't know if he was or not, but that was his excuse. I was humiliated, of course, and my *daed* was furious with me. He blamed me for driving Andrew away."

Miriam made a sympathetic sound in her throat.

"And you never told anyone?" she asked.

"Of course not." Cara heard the scorn in her own voice, and struggled to control it. "*Daed* was so angry with me after Andrew left. It wasn't until later that I realized I was pregnant. If my parents had known, they would have thrown me out of the house. Matthew's ad in *The Budget* for a bride seemed like a providential answer to so many problems." Her words became rushed. "I had no intentions of trapping him, Miriam. I—I've come to love him. He's a *gut* man, and deserves someone better than me. But what else could I do?"

"I don't know." Miriam looked troubled. "But you're going to have to confess at some point. And you're going to need prenatal care."

"I'm afraid Matthew may disown me," Cara said with as much dignity as she could. She felt tears welling up in her eyes. "In fact, I rather expect it. Miriam, i-if that happens, can you help me put the baby up for adoption?"

"*Ja*, I'm sure I can make arrangements. I have a lot of contacts within the *Englischer* medical community in Pierce."

From outside, Cara heard Matthew and Aaron talking, clearly heading for the house. "*Bitte*, don't tell anyone," gasped Cara. "Matthew mustn't know yet. I—I promise I'll tell him, but just not yet…"

"I promise," said Miriam. She jerked to her feet, scooped a small amount of the spicy chutney into a bowl and dropped a spoon into it. She slapped the bowl down on the table in front of Cara, then reached to take the baby back. "If anyone asks why you look like you're about to cry, it's because the chutney was too spicy. Got it?"

"*Ja*, got it." Cara fought back the tears even as she blessed Miriam's quick thinking.

When Matthew came into the house from Aaron's workshop, he was startled to how uncomfortable Cara looked. Her face was red and she seemed close to tears. Alarmed, he asked, "Are you okay? What's wrong?"

"Chutney," said Miriam quickly. She coughed. "Cara tasted some of the chutney I made, and it's too strong."

"*Ja.*" Cara pushed away a small bowl in front of her and wiped her eyes with her apron. "I'm afraid I have a low tolerance for spicy foods. You'll have to tone down the heat if you want this recipe to be sold in the Yoders' store," she added to Miriam.

"I can see that. I'm so sorry it made you cry," Miriam said with a strange emphasis.

Aaron coughed and rubbed his eyes.

"Even though all the windows are open, it's still pretty thick. I'm going to open both the front and back doors too. I don't want little Isaac to breathe too much of it."

"I've never had this happen before." With a rueful smile, Miriam placed the baby over her shoulder and went to open the back door. "I think I'm going to have to toss the whole batch of chutney into the compost pile."

Matthew suddenly felt his own eyes start to sting. No wonder Cara looked like she had been crying. "What kind of peppers were those, anyway?"

"Just red chili peppers," Miriam responded. "I've roasted peppers before, but never with this kind of acid cloud."

"I'm sure you're not the first to let something burn while tending to a baby," Aaron said with a gentle smile. He leaned over and kissed his wife, who blushed.

Matthew glanced at Cara and saw her face was still slightly blotchy. Well, no wonder. Sitting for any length of time in the acrid smoke would do that to anyone. But blotchy skin or not, he still thought she was the loveliest woman he'd ever seen.

Just then he coughed, hauling a handkerchief out of his pocket and mopping his eyes. "We should probably go," he told Cara. "Those peppers…"

"I'm so sorry," Miriam apologized again. "Maybe it's a *gut* thing we're going to look at that cow. It will get us out of the house long enough for the smell to fade."

"Don't worry about it," Matthew said. "You can make up for it," he teased, "by having us for dinner sometime soon. Just nothing with red peppers."

Matthew and Cara rose. While he spoke a few words to Aaron, he noticed Cara lean in to Miriam to give the new mother a hug. Miriam whispered something in Cara's ear, but he couldn't make out what was said.

A few minutes later, they were in the buggy, trotting back toward town.

"How did your discussion go with Aaron?" Cara asked. She had a handkerchief in her lap, and used it to wipe her eyes every so often.

"Fine," he said. "In fact, more than fine. Great. Aaron is so full of new ideas. He was eager to show me an improvement he'd made for his hand-milkers, an invention that he created. The man is amazing. I don't know how he thinks of the things he does. I simply can't match him for brain power."

"Your brain power is fine. Don't compare yourself." She sighed. "Sometimes I envy you, Matthew. You have so few regrets in life."

"*Ja*, true," he said thoughtfully. "I know a lot of people have done things they regretted. I can't imagine what it must be like to live with such guilt."

"It's not easy," she said, then made a gesture as if to snatch her words back.

Matthew wondered just what her former betrothed Andrew had said or done to her before he left to leave such a mental scar. "He must have hurt you badly," he murmured.

She jerked her head to face him. "How did you know?" she whispered.

"Because you told me," he replied, puzzled. "You said Andrew left you right before the wedding, *ja*?"

"Ja," she replied. Her expression shuttered. "He did."

"That's what I wonder," he continued. "Frankly, how the man can live with himself."

"I—I've wondered it myself." She turned her head to stare at the passing scenery. "He never told me why he decided he couldn't marry me. I realize now what a godsend it was, but it still stung at the time."

"Well, whatever his reasons, I intend to spend the rest of my life showing you how wrong he was to dump you." He shifted the reins to his left hand and put his other hand over hers in her lap.

Immediately she curled her fingers through his. "You're a *gut* man, Matthew," she said in a muffled tone. "I don't know what I did to deserve you, but I thank *Gott* for it."

He kept his hand entwined with hers until they approached the outskirts of town, when he needed both hands to guide the horse more precisely. He loved how open she was to small acts of intimacy. It boded well for their future.

But one thing kept nagging at him. While he understood she was glad to leave what sounded like an impossible situation in her hometown, in his opinion, her continued expressions of gratitude felt over-the-top. She seemed almost pathetically grateful for the opportunity to travel West and marry him.

But why? She was a beautiful woman. If this Andrew was a cad who threw her over, surely some other man from any of the local churches would have been happy to court her?

He was curious, but it was clearly a sensitive subject for her, and he had no wish to probe into something that might open painful wounds. So he kept his peace.

He directed the horse into the courtyard of the boardinghouse and climbed out of the buggy to unhitch. Cara also descended. "I think I'll go upstairs and take a short nap," she informed him. "That chutney upset my stomach, so I think I'll skip dinner. What time are we leaving for church tomorrow?"

He paused with his hands on the horse's bridle. "The usual time," he replied, a bit puzzled. "Nine-thirty or so."

"Ja gut." She gave him a sad smile and turned away.

He watched her as she disappeared inside the boardinghouse. When he finished unhitching the horse, he spent a little extra time grooming it and making sure it had plenty of feed and fresh water. He took some clean rags and polished the buggy, a standard practice for many men the day before a church service. And he wondered why, once again, he had imagined that there was something wrong with Cara.

Perhaps she was tired. After all, in essence she'd worked six days this week, since she had insisted on putting in some extra hours in the cannery this morning.

Well, if she could put in extra hours, so could he. It had been a couple of days since he'd done any work on the pantry he was building her. Nothing he needed to do next required any loud hammering, so he wouldn't disturb either Cara or his guest.

He walked inside, making a quick visual sweep of the lobby area to make sure everything was neat and orderly. Then he went behind the check-in desk and unlocked the door to his private quarters. Buckling on his tool belt, he got to work installing shelves in the skeletal pantry.

It took him a few minutes to realize he was still disturbed by her behavior. He got the distinct impression she was avoiding him. Why? Had he said or done something to upset her?

Women were still a mystery to him, despite growing up with three sisters and experiencing a brief previous courtship of his own. Cara was moody at times, but he didn't get the sense it was a normal state of affairs for her. Rather, it seemed she was picking at a wound somehow— sometimes it affected her, sometimes it didn't. But what could it be? Was it just normal monthly mood swings, as his sisters always experienced?

Unable to answer his own questions, he poured his energy into creating the space he knew she wanted. It was a labor of love for him, his wedding gift for her.

Briefly he wondered if she had a wedding gift in mind for him, and if so, what it could be.

It came over him like a thunderclap that

perhaps she was having second thoughts about marrying him. Did she have pre-wedding jitters? He paused in his carpentry work. Could she jilt him the way Andrew had jilted her?

He leaned his forehead against one of the pantry studs, breathing heavily. He realized he would be shattered if she changed her mind about marrying him. It made him appreciate how shattered she must have been when her fiancé left her.

But no sense borrowing trouble. He straightened up and continued his work. Unless she indicated otherwise, he would continue to pin his future hopes around a November wedding.

Chapter Thirteen

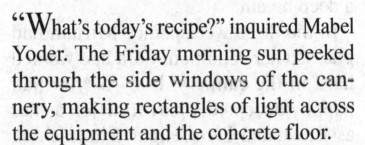

"What's today's recipe?" inquired Mabel Yoder. The Friday morning sun peeked through the side windows of the cannery, making rectangles of light across the equipment and the concrete floor.

Cara smiled at her boss. "I thought about making some more peach salsa since it sold so well the first time. I have all the ingredients, and I can have seventy-eight quarts ready to sell by tomorrow."

"*Ja gut.* I've had customers ask about it. And I assume Lucy will be in today?"

"*Ja.* Oh, Mabel, she's just a wonderful assistant. *Vielen dank* for hiring her."

"Bitte," replied Mabel. She gave Cara a thoughtful glance. "You've been looking tired lately, so I'm glad Lucy is working out. I don't want you working too hard."

Cara kept her grateful smile in place until Mabel went back to the retail store. As soon as her boss was out of sight, Cara braced her arms on one of the stainless steel counters, closed her eyes and took a deep breath.

In the three weeks since Miriam had guessed her condition, Cara had worked hard in the cannery. Lucy Naylor had happily accepted a part-time job as her assistant, and Cara delighted in teaching the older woman all the proper canning techniques. Lucy was full of good cheer. She chopped and grated and strained and peeled without complaint. She loved to gossip, but never maliciously. In fact, she was a veritable ray of sunshine in the cannery.

In contrast, Cara could feel her own sparkle diminishing. The weight of dread was pressing upon her. Just this morning, for the first time, she had felt the movement of her unborn baby within. She had subtly loosened her apron ties even further. She knew the day was fast approaching when she would need to tell Matthew about her condition. Frankly, she was surprised he hadn't already guessed. She guessed her rather tall height made the pregnancy a bit less noticeable—especially for those who had no reason to suspect anything.

Matthew was working at the boardinghouse this morning, cleaning rooms after the departure of several guests. She glanced over at the unfinished bakery area at the other end of the cannery building. He had made vast progress. The floor was laid, the half-wall railing partitioning the bakery from the cannery was in place, and several stationary work counters were almost entirely built. The woodstove was already in place, with a large metal rack holding firewood, and the

Yoders had already used the stove once or twice on cold mornings. The carpet and wingback chairs were grouped cozily around the woodstove. Cara liked the domestic touch it added.

How long she would be here to enjoy it was another question.

She was beyond grateful for Lucy's help in the last couple of weeks, because standing on her feet for eight hours a day on a concrete floor was becoming more and more difficult. She had done it at her last job—it was why she wore special cushioned shoes during the workday—but even though the developing baby was barely the size of her hand, already she could feel the effects on her body. By the end of the day, her back ached in a way it never had before.

What would she do after the baby was born? It was not like she could have an infant around in a workspace of sharp knives and pressure canners, and she wasn't qualified to do any other kind of work. More and more, she was seriously thinking about giving the baby up for adoption.

The mere thought was painful. But her child deserved to be raised by a loving family, not a desperate single mother.

She sighed and straightened up. There was no time for self-pity. She had work to do.

Pulling a two-tiered rolling cart over to where yesterday's batch of blackberry jam was already cooled and labeled, she loaded the jars onto the cart and rolled it out into the Yoders' store to stock the shelves.

"Sixty pints as usual?" inquired Thomas Kemp, the bookkeeper, as he came over to help her unload the jars onto the shelves.

"*Ja,*" she replied. "I like how people in town are starting to come in just to see what the day's product is."

"I think I once heard you say your peach salsa was your favorite. I brought a quart home to Emma, my wife, and she got hooked on it too. Next time you make a batch, I'm going to reserve two quarts for myself."

Cara laughed. "I'm making it today for just that reason." She had met Thomas's wife and two children. She also saw the family resemblance to Miriam, since Thomas was her brother. As such, she could hardly help but like the bookkeeper. "Tell Emma it's easy to make. I can give her the recipe."

"*Danke*, I'm sure she'd like that." He pulled a notebook out of the pocket of his canvas work apron, made a notation about the jam and returned to his office.

Back in the cannery, Cara began following the recipe for a batch of peach salsa. This was the portion of canning that normally soothed her—prepping the ingredients—but today her nerves were rattled and a headache tugged at the corners of her forehead. Maybe it was because the time to confess her condition to Matthew was imminent.

The bell peppers in front of her on the chopping block blurred, and she forced the tears back. She felt a growing love for the small human developing inside her. It would grieve her to give the baby to another family to raise, but she could then begin her life anew.

A noise at the connecting door made her look up. Matthew walked through, and his face lit up with a smile when he saw her. For his sake, she tamped down her fears and returned with a smile of her own.

"Guten tag," she said. "Are the rooms all clean?"

"Ja, and the boardinghouse is empty at the moment. No guests for a couple days, so I can put in some extra time here." He gestured toward the other end of the large cannery building. "A few more days, and Abe likely can start ordering some of the equipment for the bakery, such as the ovens."

Watching his face, Cara had a sudden

realization: she loved Matthew. She loved him deeply. The thought of his reaction when he learned the truth worried her greatly.

Matthew strode toward the other end of the cannery building and picked up his tool belt, which he clipped on. Humming, he got to work.

These were the times Cara cherished. She loved it when Matthew was with her, working on something separate but nearby. She loved the running conversations they so often had across the width of the building.

It was little things like this she knew she would miss if Matthew broke off their courtship. But there was so much more. The companionable times over the breakfast table as he made her his specialty omelet. The times they worked together to clean a room or check in a guest. Watching him work as he neared completion on the beautiful pantry he was building her. The cozy dinner conversations when the day's work was behind them, as they told each other about childhood anecdotes or trivial incidences.

In other words, she would miss his courtship. She knew Matthew would make some woman a wonderful *hutband*; unfortunately, she was growing to think it was less and less likely that woman would be her.

Three hours later, she used the jar-lifter to pull the superheated quarts of peach salsa from the pressure canners and set them on racks to cool.

"Well, that's about all I can get done today," she told Matthew. She washed her hands and dried them on a towel. "How about you?"

"*Ja*, I think I could call it a day." He unhooked his tool belt and hung it on a chair back.

Cara started to arch backward to stretch out her aching back, but stopped herself quickly. Such an action would only make her stomach more prominent. Instead, she walked over and plucked her cloak off its hook near the connecting door and donned it, pulling the folds in front of her to hide her thickening middle.

Matthew shrugged himself into his coat. "Ready?"

"Ja." She preceded him through the connecting door, said good night to the Yoders and stepped out into the street where the sun shone low.

"It's easy to tell winter is coming," Matthew remarked, adjusting a scarf around his neck. "The Yoders got another load of firewood delivered, stacked in the alley behind the store. It should be enough to heat both the store and the cannery over the winter."

"Gut. Often I get so warm working around the canners I don't need any extra heat, but the Yoders have used the stove a few times in the morning to take the chill off the inside of the building."

She shivered. It wasn't so much from the chilly air as from the realization that the time was coming when she must tell Matthew her secret.

"Cold?" he asked. Always he was observant about her comfort.

"Ja. Nein," she contradicted, then sighed. "Sometimes it's hard to decide."

"Cara, are you *oll recht*?" Matthew asked gently.

She fought back the sudden stinging in her eyes and kept her gaze on the sidewalk in front of her. *"Ja,* sure," she replied. "What could be wrong?"

It had been subtle at first, but now it was unmistakable: Cara was different.

It was hard to pinpoint exactly how, but at some level Matthew knew she was fighting to keep a cheerful front, but he saw through the effort to the troubled woman underneath.

Unable quite to identify the issue, he found himself talking more just to try and draw her out, to encourage her to unburden herself, to let him help.

And of course, he examined himself. Was it something he'd done? Didn't do? Said? Didn't say? What? He was baffled, puzzled.

Several times over the past few weeks, he'd asked her if anything was the matter. Invariably she said *"Nein,"* and turned away to do something innocuous—fiddle with the strings of her *kapp*, needlessly brush invisible crumbs from a surface, polish something with a corner of her apron.

When had she changed? Though it was hard to put a finger on the exact date, he noticed she had been quieter and more subdued ever since their visit with Miriam and Aaron. Had Miriam said something to upset her? Miriam was a *gut* woman, confident and tactful, not subject to gossip or malicious talk, so Matthew couldn't imagine she had said anything offensive or hurtful.

The vivacious woman he had been falling in love with had suddenly turned moody and withdrawn, and as best he could figure, it stemmed from that one visit. What happened?

Tonight, as always, he tried to keep things normal. "How do you feel about a ground beef and cabbage skillet? I have a cabbage in the icebox, and you still have some jars of ground beef canned up."

"*Ja*, that sounds gut." Cara removed her cloak. "And I have a hankering for some onion patties, too. I'll make them."

This, too, was part of their normal routine. Each contributed something toward dinner. He enjoyed cooking, and he knew she did too. They were learning each other's favorite dishes. They sometimes experimented, using whatever ingredients were on hand to create a spontaneous meal.

But tonight, though she was just as willing to prepare food, she did so with a down-turned face and flattened voice.

While he started a fire in the wood cookstove, she fetched the jars of canned ground beef and tomato sauce from the nearly finished pantry. "I'll chop the onions," she offered.

"*Ja gut.* And I'll chop the cabbage."

The room warmed as they worked on opposite sides of the table. Wanting to fill the silence, he started a stream of chatter. He told her about the guests who had checked out and of the book one of them had left behind, which he intended to mail out next week. He mentioned the new quilt he had purchased to replace a worn one in one of the rooms. He related Abe Yoder's plans for the bakery.

The room filled with the delicious smell of cooking food. Matthew started assembling the skillet meal. He looked at Cara, busy chopping onions, and saw tears streaming down her cheeks.

"Strong onion?" he observed.

"*Ja.*" She paused to wipe her eyes with her apron, and gave an inelegant sniff. "But onion patties are so *gut*, it's worth it."

The quip failed to disguise what seemed an uneasy reality. Her tears were not caused solely by the onions.

"Cara, is anything wrong?" he asked gently. Again.

"Nein." She said the word quickly, and he knew with surety that she lied. But what could he do? He couldn't force an answer from her.

He turned away, troubled. Perhaps getting married in November wasn't such a good idea after all. Whatever her problem, he shouldn't put himself in a position to be irrevocably yoked with her until he knew if it would impact their future happiness.

She poured some oil into a cast-iron skillet and let it heat while she formed onion patties. When the oil was hot, she dropped them in one by one and let them cook until they were a golden brown. Meanwhile, he kept his own pan covered so the skillet meal would cook and combine the flavors. While she attended to the stove, he set the table.

When the meal was ready, he paused to silently ask for a blessing, as did she. But Matthew's prayer was more than thanksgiving for the food. Instead, he asked for strength and guidance. After dinner, he intended to force the issue. The uncertainty must stop.

He waited until she had finished eating. When she rose to start clearing away the dishes, he stopped her. "Cara, we have to talk."

She stared at him with wide eyes. "About what?"

"I need to know what's bothering you."

"What makes you think something is bothering me?"

"Don't tell falsehoods, Cara." He kept any rancor out of his voice. "It's as plain as the nose on your face."

She dropped back into her chair and buried her face in her hands. There was silence in the room, broken only by the ticking of the kitchen clock.

"You've changed over the last few weeks," he prompted. "The vivacious and enthusiastic woman I fell in love with is gone. I need to know why."

"I meant to tell you earlier," she mumbled through her hands, still hiding her face. "I just couldn't muster up the courage."

He started to feel alarmed. "What is it? Do you have a fatal disease or something?"

"*Nein...*"

He waited, but no more information was forthcoming. Matthew started to feel irritation. "Well, if you're not ill, what's the matter?"

She jerked to her feet and whirled away from the table. To his surprise, she began clearing the kitchen: putting pans in the sink, scraping the leftover skillet meal into a container to put in the icebox. He sat, dumbfounded, watching her frantic avoidance activity.

Finally he rose and took her by the shoulders, making her turn around to face him. She refused to meet his eyes, instead staring at the floor. "Cara, please talk to me. I have to know what's going on. I can't proceed with this courtship until I know why you're depressed."

"Y-You're going to be furious."

"I might be," he conceded. "But I still have to know what it is. Is it something I did?"

"Nein!" She jerked free and turned her back on him. "It's nothing you did. In fact, you've been wonderful. Almost too wonderful. It just makes it harder."

"Makes *what* harder?" She was talking in riddles and he wanted her to get to the point.

There was a few moments' silence, during which he heard her labored breathing punctuated by tiny inarticulate sounds, like a hurt kitten. He stared at her bowed back. What could be so bad that it caused her almost physical pain to confess it? "Cara, talk to me," he repeated.

"It—it was a calculated gamble to come out here to Montana," she choked at last. "But you know what my home life was like. I was anxious to get away from my parents, and away from my church community after the humiliation of being left by Andrew. But there's something I couldn't tell my parents and certainly couldn't tell you."

"Then tell me and get it over with."

She broke down crying, an ugly harsh sound. Matthew pulled her into his arms. She leaned into him, her face contorted and ravaged, weeping as if someone had died. He knew he wouldn't be able to get a coherent word out of her in this state, so he simply held her, rocking her gently to and fro, feeling her tears soak through the shoulder of his shirt.

"Ich k-kann dich nicht heiraten," she finally choked out. "I c-can't marry you."

He felt a cold chill down his spine. In that instant he realized how much he loved her, how much he looked forward to sharing his future with her. All the little domestic habits they'd fallen into over the past few months had become dear and cherished. And now she was saying she couldn't marry him?

He pressed her *kapp*, hugging her closer, continuing to act as a rock during her distress. Whatever her reasons for saying that devastating sentence, he was sure they could work it out. He didn't want to give her up.

"Why do you say that?" he finally asked, even though her storm of weeping was nowhere near finished. "Whatever the matter is, can't we talk it through?"

"N-nein," she stuttered, and sobbed some more. "Y-you won't want to marry me after what I have to t-tell you."

He fished into his pocket and pulled out

a clean handkerchief, which he handed her. She nodded and held it to her face, mopping her streaming eyes while still encased in his protected embrace.

It took a long time for the strident weeping to fade. All the while, he continued to hold her, willing his strength to flow into hers, grasping desperately in his mind for what awful thing she had to confess that would prevent them from getting married.

Finally she came to a hiccupping silence, leaning into him, her cheek against his soaked shirt and the handkerchief pressed against her face.

"Komm," he said gently, turning her toward the living room area where they could be seated. *"Komm* over here. We can work through this, Cara, but I have to know what it is. The time for secrecy is over."

He pressed her down into a comfortable chair, then yanked another chair close by so he could continue to offer support.

She sat in the chair, twisting the handkerchief with both hands, her head bowed. "Tell me," he urged again.

Finally she lifted her head and met his eyes, her own eyes red and swollen. "I'm going to have a baby."

Chapter Fourteen

Cara watched the blood drain from Matthew's face. She'd known this day would come. She just hadn't expected it to come so soon. Miriam's clever guesswork had forced her hand sooner than she wanted, yet in some ways it was a relief to have her secret out in the open. She was definitely starting to show; there was no way she could fool Matthew for much longer.

"A baby," he stated in a cold, flat tone. His eyes flicked down to her midsection, then returned to her face.

"*J-ja,*" she hiccuped. "I'm four months along, almost five. Obviously I've been doing my best to hide it, but Miriam guessed. She told me I would have to tell you before we got married. I meant to, Matthew, *Gott* knows I meant to…but somehow I kept putting it off."

The tears came again, but this time Matthew made no move to comfort her. Cara buried her face in the handkerchief, too ashamed to look at him. Suddenly she felt very, very alone.

"Who was it?" he asked at last. He leaned back in his chair and crossed his arms.

"It was Andrew," she said. She met his eyes, looking like chips of flint, and skittered her glance away. "It was before he left me."

"You got pregnant by your former fiancé?"

"*Ja.*"

Cara composed herself, wiped her eyes and lifted her chin.

"Andrew was persuasive. He kept pressuring me to…to be intimate before the wedding, especially since it was so close. What difference would a couple weeks make, after all? That's what he said."

She took a deep breath. "Afterwards, his attitude changed. It's like…he got what he wanted, and then he didn't want me anymore, even though the whole wedding was already planned. He s-started disappearing for longer and longer stretches of time. I k-kept trying to pretend everything was fine, but I knew nothing was the same. When he finally t-told me he wanted to break it off, it didn't surprise me. It was almost a r-relief."

"A relief?" prompted Matthew.

She glanced at him. He was listening intently, though a thundercloud still rested on his brow.

"*Ja*, a relief. He had changed so much in a short space of time, and I didn't like what I saw. I f-felt desolate. My grandmother was gone. The man who was courting me was gone. It didn't help that my *daed* kept blaming me for Andrew's desertion. I was depressed and desperate. Then w-within a few weeks, I knew I was in even worse trouble."

"Andrew never knew you were pregnant?"

"*Nein.* By that point he had moved to another community, and rumor had it he was courting someone else."

"And you knew you were pregnant when you answered my ad in *The Budget*?"

"I was so ashamed of what happened. I could hardly show my face in town or at church, even though I told no one."

"So you thought you'd found a pushover, someone who would give your baby a name."

"I thought *Gott* had given me a solution," she replied with dignity. "I knew I'd have to tell you at some point. It's not like this could be disguised forever. But I'd hoped…hoped…" Her voice trailed off.

There was silence in the room except for the ticking clock. What *had* she hoped for? That Matthew would be her knight in shining armor, rescuing her from her predicament? Putting her vague dreams into words seemed inadequate somehow.

"Go on," said Matthew coldly. "What did you hope for?"

"Rescue, I suppose." She sighed. "But don't worry, I'm not asking you to do that. It's too much to ask of anyone. I've already spoken to Miriam. She's going to help me p-put the baby up for adoption." Verbalizing it somehow made the difficult choice more real—and more difficult. "I know I won't be able to work in the cannery with an infant. The only possible solution is to give the baby to someone else to raise."

"It sounds like you've thought through every possible contingency," Matthew said in that same frozen voice. "Except the contingency of how I would react."

"Believe me, Matthew, I've thought through that too. I had no choice. I had to think through *everything*."

"Then why didn't you tell me?" he burst out in an anguished voice. "Why didn't you tell me sooner?"

"When?" she snapped back. She dropped into sarcasm. "Straight off when we met? *'Guten tag*, Matthew, it's nice to meet you, and oh yeah, I'm expecting another man's baby.' That would have gone over well, don't you think?"

"Then when did you plan to tell me?"

"Soon. Obviously I had no choice. But I—I wanted to get to know you. Were you like Andrew? Were you like my *daed*? You were completely unknown to me. I had no one I could ask as a character reference. Put yourself in my shoes, Matthew. Alone, frightened, pregnant, with no one I could turn to for support or strength. I've had to depend on myself. Thanks to you, I was able to flee what might have become an abusive situation under my father's roof. I was able to turn my back to a church community that whispered behind their hands and gave me pitying looks after Andrew left. How much worse would it have been to have an out-of-wedlock baby there?"

"And how you're having an out-of-wedlock baby here," he retorted. "What's the saying? 'Out of the frying pan, into the fire.'"

"Ja und nein," she said. "Somehow it's easier here. I don't have a lifetime of connections with the people in this community as I did in my old one. If my reputation is shredded once my condition is known, then it's shredded. But if it gets too hard, I know now I can move somewhere else and start over again. *Ja,* Matthew, I've thought it all through."

"And where do I fit into all these plans of yours?"

She looked at him, noticing for the first time the lines of suffering around his mouth. "I don't know. You tell me."

He dropped his head in his hands. "I don't know either. All I know is this isn't what I hoped for when you answered my ad and traveled to Montana to become my wife. I wanted children, *ja*, but *ours*, not someone else's."

"What's done is done, Matthew." Cara felt courage rising. She was suddenly able to step outside her emotions and examine the situation with detachment. "I can't change what happened. The only thing I can do is apologize for not telling you sooner, then make my future plans— without you, if necessary."

He raised his head, and looked at her. "All this while I've just been a tool in your plans, offering you a free place to stay, as well as my good name. But all the while you were planning on foisting someone else's baby on me."

"If you put it that way, *ja*. I suppose I did see you as a means to an end. But it wasn't done out of malice, Matthew. It was done out of desperation. What else would you have had me do?"

"Stay in your old church and take your licks," he snapped.

She nodded. "I suppose if this has done nothing else, it's revealed the true character of both of us. You see me as a calculating woman who used you for my own ends. And now I'm seeing you as a harsh man unable to understand what it's like to be trapped."

He sprang to his feet and began pacing. Finally he whirled around and faced her. "And what would you have me do now?" he almost shouted. "Say it doesn't matter? Say I'll raise the baby as my own? Say I don't mind that you deceived me literally from the first time we communicated?"

"It's just as I anticipated," she said, lifting her chin. "I'm on my own. I understand that now."

"I don't know why you expected anything else," he gritted. "Ironically, this is why my parents objected to a mail-order bride. Almost an identical thing happened to my uncle many years ago, and he never got over it. This is as low a blow as I could ever expect from anyone, much less the woman I thought was going to be my wife." He turned his back to her, and she watched his hands form into fists. "It's over, Cara. It's over."

Matthew tried to keep from hyperventilating. The anger coursing through his body made his pulse pound and his fists clench. Did Cara really think she could trick him into marrying her to provide a name for her baby?

Conflict struggled within him. The idea of the perfect wife warred with the image of the very imperfect woman who had wept before him.

"I feel betrayed," he ground out at last. "Betrayed—and, maybe, angry at *Gott*."

"I know you do." Despite her ravaged face, somehow she looked beautiful at that moment. He realized it was because she had an innate dignity that transcended her problems.

But dignity couldn't bandage over the harsh reality of her thickened figure, mute testimony that she was carrying another man's baby.

He couldn't stay any longer, not until he cooled down—otherwise he might say something he would regret later on. Snatching his heavy coat off the hook by the door, he walked out of his private quarters, through the boardinghouse lobby, and out into the courtyard.

The subdued sounds of the darkened town came to him. It was early evening and most businesses were closed. Pierce was seldom a noisy place, and on this quiet Friday night, he heard nothing more than the swish of ordinary traffic. If the sounds of the town could reflect what he was feeling inside, he thought grimly, he should be hearing fireworks. Instead, he heard the chirp of crickets from a corner near the stable.

Restless and needing to burn off his anger, he walked toward the town's park, two blocks away. Stars shone overhead, dimmed somewhat by streetlights. The large trees in the park had dropped their leaves, and already civic-minded towns-people had wrapped the trunks with colorful lights in preparation for the hol-idays, though the lighting ceremony had not yet taken place. Each tree was spon-sored by a business in town, and when lit up in November and December, the park was beautiful.

But now it was dark and deserted, per-fectly suiting his mood.

He paced back and forth, his feet crunching on the finely graveled path-ways that crisscrossed the green space, wondering what to do. He felt like the rug had been yanked out from under him. He could hardly think straight, trying to di-gest the overwhelming news.

Everything he had planned for was gone in an instant. The wife he thought he would have was gone. The future ba-bies—his babies—he hoped to have were gone. Everything was gone. What was left except a lonely bachelor existence?

"Why, *Gott*, why?" he cried to the skies, literally shaking a fist at the stars. How could *Gott* betray him like this? How could *Gott* give him such hope and the promise of such a wonderful woman to be his wife, only to snatch it away?

One thing was certain: he should have listened to his parents' concerns when he'd placed the advertisement for a mail-order bride in *The Budget*.

He sat down on a bench and dropped his head in his hands, utterly unable to figure out what to do next. He felt frozen.

His parents. They would be furious, of course; and if he continued his courtship of a pregnant woman, they likely would follow up on their threat to boot him from his job and home at the boardinghouse.

What then? Abe Yoder's kindly offer to retrofit the bakery area into temporary housing was the only solution he could think of.

He needed to talk to someone, but who? Not his parents; they already were suspi-

cious. Not his brother Mark, who might
be inclined to say, "I told you so" since he
had also expressed concerns about advertising for a wife. Not his sister Eva, who
was eager to embrace Cara as a sibling.

The bishop? Yes, he could talk to the
bishop. It was his job to listen to the concerns of church members, and offer counsel. And counsel was something Matthew
needed very badly right now.

Matthew stood up and began walking. It
was three miles to the bishop's house, located well out of town and into the Amish
settlement. Matthew didn't have a lantern
or a flashlight, but he had enough streetlights to see him to the edge of town, and
then starlight and a half-moon to illumi-
nate the rest of the way. Pierce was small
enough that it ended abruptly, with very
little sprawl.

It took him an hour to walk the distance. He shuffled along, his eyes on the
dark ground, his thoughts running this

way and that, chaotically, like a squirrel trapped in a box. What should he do?

He heard a great horned owl hoot from the blackness of some pine trees off the road. From a distance away, he heard a higher-pitched hoot, that of the owl's mate. Even the owls were paired off, Matthew thought sourly. It seemed everyone had a partner except him.

The night was cold. Matthew adjusted the collar of his coat closer around his neck and wished for a scarf and a pair of gloves. The fury that had pumped heat through his veins was cooling into cold anger.

At last he saw the bishop's house before him. In the light of the half-moon, the window in the living room softly glowed, and he could see smoke rising from a stovepipe.

Matthew paused, shoved his chilly hands in his coat pockets and stared at the window. Doubtless the bishop and his wife were quietly reading or chatting, enjoying the typical after-dinner indoor activities so many older happily married couples engaged in. It was that kind of future he had envisioned with Cara, one of quiet domestic tranquility.

But no more. That possibility had been snatched out from underneath him.

In a moment of insight, he recognized part of his anger stemmed from the grief of knowing that future was no longer a possibility with Cara. He would never share the soft light of an oil lamp while reading or chatting or anything else. And it *was* grief, he realized—the grief of losing something that he knew had been very dear to him.

He sighed. His anger was ebbing, which was good. He could hardly expect the bishop to understand the fury that had enveloped him at Cara's confession. He took a deep breath and walked up the pathway to the bishop's house. His knock sounded very loud in the quiet evening darkness.

There was a moment's pause. Matthew

could well imagine the startled looks between the bishop and his wife, the soft exclamation at the disruption. After a few moments, from inside the house Matthew heard footsteps approaching the door. The bishop spoke through the heavy wood. "*Wer ist da?* Who is it?"

"Matthew Miller," Matthew said. "May I talk with you?"

The door opened, and Samuel Beiler stared at him by the light of the oil lamp he held in one hand. "Matthew! Is everything all right? Why are you out so late?"

"*Nein*, everything is *not* all right, and I'm sorry to bother you this late. Bishop Beiler, I need someone to talk to. Do you have time?"

"*Ja*, sure, of course." The older man stepped aside and made a motion of welcome. Then he peered outside. "Where's your horse? Or did you walk all the way here?"

"I walked." Matthew stepped over the

threshold and made to remove his hat until he realized he wasn't wearing one.

Lois Beiler stood in the living room, a look of concern on her face. "*Gut'n owed*, Matthew," she said. "I hope it's nothing too serious?"

Matthew looked from Lois to Samuel Beiler and saw the worry in their kindly faces, and he felt his own face crumple as he struggled to fight the unexpected pressure of tears.

Samuel Beiler made an exclamation. "*Ach!* Matthew, sit down, let us know what happened. Did someone die?"

Not some*one*, thought Matthew, but some*thing*. Namely, his dreams. "*Nein...*" he choked.

"Should I leave?" Lois inquired with her usual discretion. "If you need to talk privately, that is."

"*N-nein,*" Matthew stuttered. "Having a woman's perspective would probably be a *gut* thing."

"Let me take your coat," Samuel Beiler

said. "And *lieb*—" He turned to his wife. "Could you bring some coffee? I think there's some in the carafe on the counter."

"*Ja*, sure." The older woman slipped away toward the kitchen.

The bishop placed the oil lamp he had been carrying on a small table while Matthew shrugged off his coat. The church leader took the garment and hung it on a peg near the door, then gestured toward the living room. "*Bitte*, come sit down."

Matthew stumbled toward the living room. It was as he predicted. The room was warmly lit up with two lamps. A crackling woodstove put out heat. A knitting basket with an abandoned project occupied one chair. A history book rested on a small stand by another chair. A cat blinked at him from a footstool. In some ways the cozy domestic scene was like a knife in Matthew's heart, reminding him of the future he'd lost.

"Sit here," the bishop said.

Matthew snapped out of his momentary daze and dropped into the seat indicated. The bishop pulled over a small coffee table just as Lois came out of the kitchen with a tray holding a carafe and three mugs, along with cream, sugar and spoons.

She placed the tray on the coffee table and poured Matthew a cup of coffee. "Cream or sugar?" she inquired.

"Nein, danke." Matthew gave a small, bitter laugh. "Black coffee suits my mood right now."

The older woman nodded warily, removed the knitting from her chair and sat down.

The bishop poured himself a mug of coffee, spooned in some sugar and added a dollop of cream. Then he sat back, stirring the beverage. "Now tell us what happened. I've never seen you in such distress, Matthew. But you said no one has died?"

"*Nein*. The only thing that's died is my dreams." He took a deep, shuddering breath. "Cara is not who she seems."

Chapter Fifteen

When Matthew turned his back on her and stalked away, it was possibly the worst moment of Cara's life—possibly even worse than when she'd realized she was pregnant.

In a blinding moment, she understood how much she had come to trust, depend on and—yes—love Matthew. What would she do without him?

She'd thought she was ready for this moment. Now that the moment was here, she wasn't so sure. She slouched down in the chair and dropped her head against the backrest. Closing her eyes, she tried to pray, but words wouldn't come.

She felt the baby move within her, faintly, like the brush of a butterfly's wings. "Am I upsetting you, *liebling*?" she asked, cupping her expanding middle with two hands. She knew very well a mother's emotional state could impact an unborn baby's development, and she strove for calm.

She hoisted herself to her feet. Matthew's wedding present to her, the beautiful pantry, mocked her with how close it was to completion. She stepped inside the dark interior. The shelves gleamed faintly. The metal flour bin caught a ray of the kitchen's oil lamp, and the few jars of canned meat she had placed inside taunted her with the potential for seeing so much more. But it was over. That was what Matthew had said.

This little storage room, the silent testimony of his love for her—the wedding present custom-made to demonstrate his feelings—was no longer hers. She turned away. Someday in the future, Matthew would marry someone else. Cara hoped his future wife would appreciate such a beautiful pantry.

She stood at the window overlooking the dark, enclosed backyard. The bird feeders, which Matthew said he preferred to fill only in the colder months, were faintly lit up by the streetlights a block away. She regretted never having a chance to see what feathered creatures would be attracted to the food, of sitting next to him by the windows with little binoculars and identifying the species. All the little regrets that came with ending a relationship...

She could run away. Pack her suitcases, catch a bus and disappear, never to be seen again. But she knew it wasn't a viable option. Not anymore. No, the best choice was to give the baby up for adoption. Miriam had said she would help when the time came. *Then* she could run away, move to another Amish community and start over.

In the meantime…she didn't belong here. She no longer had the right to live free of charge in Matthew's boardinghouse. She wasn't quite sure where to go, but she seriously doubted he would want her to stay.

She dragged herself up the stairs to her room. There were no other guests tonight. No sounds of people talking or listening to music, no opening or closing of doors as visitors came and went. No underlying sense of other people around. The large building seemed to echo and press her down with its weight.

She stepped into the room that had been her home for so many happy weeks of getting to know Matthew. For the most part, it was neat and tidy. Every day she made sure the bed was made, and she left no personal belongings scattered carelessly about. It didn't take long to pack her suitcases.

While she folded clothes and tucked away books and other items, she wondered where to go. It was not like she could spend the night on the street. It was too far to walk to the settlement. What should she do?

The answer rose smooth and unprompted into her mind: *the cannery*. Of course. She had a key to the outside street door. The mercantile was closed for the night, and no one would disturb her. The chairs and carpet the Yoders had purchased—and which she and Matthew had chosen—made for a cozy and inviting oasis. She had even joked once about the chairs being comfortable enough to sleep on. She would spend the night in the cannery, and tomorrow she would figure out what to do next.

Meanwhile, she wanted to erase the evidence of her presence as thoroughly as possible. She gave the room and bathroom a fast cleaning. Then one by one she took her suitcases downstairs and loaded them on one of the luggage carts Matthew used to accommodate guests. She would return the cart later.

Then she laid her room key on the front desk where Matthew was sure to see it. She hoped he understood what it meant.

She opened the boardinghouse door, stepped outside, pulled the luggage cart after her and locked the door behind her. She would return the rest of the building's keys when she returned the luggage cart.

The night was chilly. Standing in the courtyard, protected from prying eyes and even streetlights from the rest of the town, she glanced upward and saw stars and a half-moon illuminating the night. "*Bitte, Gott*, forgive me," she whispered. She pulled the edges of her cloak closer around her neck, gripped the handle of the luggage cart and started walking toward the cannery.

"What do you mean, Cara is not what she seems?" queried the bishop, a look of bewilderment on his face.

Matthew gave a harsh bark of mirthless laughter. "Just what I said. Bishop, she lied to me even before we met. She's pregnant."

Both Samuel and Lois Beiler sucked in their breaths with identical shocked expressions. A momentary silence descended on the room. Lois made a tiny mewling sound of pity.

A detached part of Matthew admired the bishop for his stoic calmness, especially at a time when he himself felt so agitated. Samuel Beiler took a small sip of coffee.

"And I assume you had nothing to do with this?" he asked.

"Of course not." Matthew felt cold anger inside at the question.

"Forgive me, but I just needed to make sure I have my facts straight." The church leader cradled his coffee mug with both hands. "I understand this is a serious development. Has she explained the circumstances under which this occurred?"

"*Ja*. Here's what she told me..." Matthew related the story Cara had given him. He did his best to keep anger out of his voice, but it wasn't easy.

When he was finished, the bishop was silent for a moment, then said, "I understand your anger, Matthew. But imagine if such a thing had happened to one of your sisters."

"But...but...don't you think she should have told me from the start?"

"And when would have been the best time to tell you?"

"Any time!" Matthew exploded. "I should have had all the facts ahead of time! She was pregnant when she answered my ad in *The Budget*, though she tells me she had every intention of telling me before the wedding. It's not like she could disguise it much longer anyway. But I should have been able to know this from the start!"

"Do you know why she might have delayed telling you?"

324 The Amish Bride's Secret

"I imagine she knew I would be far less likely to want to marry her."

"*Ja*, I think that was a lot of it. Can you blame her?"

"Maybe not, but what about me? I laid the moon and stars at her feet. I was ready to share everything with her, including my life!"

"Matthew, this isn't just about you." Bishop Beiler locked eyes with him. "Stop focusing on what *you* want, what *you* expected. If you are ever to be a married man, you need to consider the other person more than yourself. Put yourself in Cara's shoes. What else could she have done?"

"She could have told me!" Matthew repeated a bit less forcefully. He realized he was beginning to sound like a petulant child.

The older man's eyebrows rose. "She just did."

Again, the church leader's quiet statement stopped Matthew in his tracks. He slumped in his chair. "*Ja*, she did."

"Matthew..." Lois Beiler placed her coffee mug back on the tray and clasped her hands in her lap. "All shock and dismay aside, what are your feelings toward Cara?"

"I love her," Matthew admitted. "I think I have from the start. But this is something I didn't anticipate. I honestly don't know what to do."

"For starters, I suggest you wait until next year to get married," Samuel Beiler said. "But one thing is certain. Cara and her baby are a package deal. If you feel you can't marry her, that's fine. Set her free. But if you feel you *can* marry her despite her condition, then you *must* accept the baby as yours, and never treat it differently than any of your future children. Is that clear?"

The bishop's words made sense, even if Matthew wasn't overly eager to hear them. But wasn't that what he came here for? Counseling?

"That's fair." Matthew stared at his coffee mug. "But I don't yet know if I still want to marry her. At any rate, I see the wisdom of waiting until next year. Meanwhile, she'll have the unpleasant experience of being a single mother." Under his breath, he added, "Serves her right."

Bishop Beiler shook his head and his expression became stern again. "Matthew, stop it. That's just the kind of hostile attitude I'm warning against."

"I know, but…"

"There is no 'but.' 'Let he who is without sin cast the first stone.' You're casting stones, Matthew, where none are deserved. You are not a sinless man. Neither am I. None of us are. Cara may have waited longer than she should have to tell you her condition, and she should have known better than to engage in premarital relations—especially as a baptized member of the church—but it sounds like she bitterly regrets her decision."

Matthew remained slumped in the chair. "So you think I should marry her."

"*Nein*, I didn't say that. I'm saying you should stop *blaming* her."

He blew out a breath of frustration and stared at his coffee cup. Was that what he was doing? Blaming her? Yet how could he overlook her condition and get married as if nothing was wrong?

He realized he was still grieving. Cara's confession had killed his fantasy of a perfect wife and a perfect life.

How did things get so complicated? The woman he had once courted had dumped him, citing the difficulties in leaving behind her extended family to move to Montana. It had taken a while, but he got over it.

But since then, time had gone by and he was still single. He wanted nothing more than to be a devoted family man, with a wife and—someday—children of his own. Why was it so hard to achieve this simple goal?

The idea of putting an ad in *The Budget* had come to him in the dead of night. He had attributed the inspiration to *Gott*, which was why he'd followed through despite his parents' opposition. His prayers for a wife had been answered by what'd seemed like the perfect woman—who turned out to be not so perfect after all.

His parents would be furious.

"I guess I have some serious thinking to do," he finally concluded out loud.

"*Ja*, and some serious praying to do," the bishop said. His voice gentled. "Your news about Cara's condition was a blow to Lois and me. I can only imagine how much bigger a blow it was to you."

"That's for sure," muttered Matthew.

"So *ja*, you have a lot to think about," continued the church leader, "but consider a few things. Cara is a lovely woman, both inside and out. Up until this point, you had no doubts about courting her.

While her pregnancy changes the immediate future, it doesn't change *her*. She's the same person you fell in love with. She also has hopes and dreams about the future, just as you did, and this threw an enormous monkey wrench into those plans—just as much for her as for you."

"She mentioned giving the baby up for adoption," admitted Matthew.

"That would certainly be an option," agreed the bishop. "But here's another thing to consider. No matter the circumstances under which she got pregnant, the baby is innocent, and Cara knows that. Giving the baby up for adoption might be a logical solution, but it would tear her heart out. So if you suggest giving the baby up for adoption *as a condition* for marrying you, she may agree—but she will come to resent you for it. Trust me on that, I've seen it before."

Matthew was startled. "That never occurred to me!" he exclaimed. "I would never suggest she give her baby away for that reason!"

"That's *gut*, then." The bishop smiled. "If you decide not to marry her and she opts to give the baby away, that's a different issue. But as I said before, if you continue your courtship, she and her baby are a package deal."

Matthew exhaled. "Agreed. I don't know what *Gott* wants me to do yet, Bishop Beiler, but I appreciate your insight." He looked at Lois. "And yours too."

The bishop's wife smiled. "Speaking as a woman, I'm inclined to be sympathetic toward Cara. She was scared and desperate, Matthew, and likely that's why she didn't confess she was pregnant until now. Being pregnant means hormones she's never experienced before are circulating through her body. It alters the way women think. Whatever logic she used to answer your ad and travel to Montana might have been based purely on desperate emotion. Don't judge her too harshly or hold that against her."

Matthew placed his nearly full mug of coffee back on the tray. "I'll take your word for it." He sighed and stood up. "*Vielen dank*, both of you. I'm sorry to burst in on you this late in the evening."

"It's what I'm here for, Matthew." The bishop also stood up, and clasped Matthew on the shoulder. "Go home and pray about it. We're here if you want to talk some more."

Feeling calmer—though no less certain what to do—Matthew donned his coat and started the long walk back to town. It gave him time to think…and pray.

His anger had died out. Lois's final comments were helpful. Matthew knew Cara didn't get support from her family back in Pennsylvania. Had her parents learned of her pregnancy, they might well have disowned her. No wonder she'd answered his advertisement and kept her condition a secret.

But could he truly raise another man's child? He thought of all the people in his church back East—and for that matter, here in Montana—where people had done just that. Some had adopted children. Some had married a widow or widower and stepped in as a stepparent. And yes, he vaguely recalled a man from his old church who had married a woman who was pregnant from a premarital fling. To the best of his knowledge, they were happy and he had raised the resulting child as his own without a problem.

But his uncle hadn't. His uncle had moved to another state and remained a bachelor for the rest of his life.

Cara's confession made him realize he was not the generous or accepting man he had always prided himself on being. There was nothing like being tested to throw such pride back in one's face. Maybe this was *Gott's* way of keeping him humble.

The night was chilly. Matthew turned

up the collar of his coat. The crunch of gravel beneath his feet sounded loud, but his eyes adjusted to the night's darkness and he had no trouble navigating his way back to town.

He approached the boardinghouse, looming large and dark before him, and stopped for a moment, looking up at Cara's room window. It was dark. Perhaps she had already gone to bed, no doubt exhausted by the emotions of the evening. He felt weary himself, and nowhere closer to having an answer.

Sighing, he went through the courtyard and turned the handle of the door. It was locked.

Baffled, he stepped back a moment and wondered why she had locked the building. Normally he only locked it if there were no guests present. But there was one guest in residence: Cara herself. Why would she lock the door?

He hadn't thought to bring his keys with him when he stormed out in a temper a couple hours ago. Fortunately he kept a spare key hidden in the stable, which he fetched.

The lobby was dark. Matthew made his way to the front desk and withdrew the oil lamp and matches he kept in a cabinet below. He lit the lamp and went through the door to his private quarters, which was unlocked.

She wasn't there. The remains of the fire in the cookstove meant the room was warm, but Cara wasn't there.

She might be hiding in her room, but they needed to talk. Matthew took the lamp, climbed the stairs to the second floor and knocked on her room door.

Silence.

Was she asleep? Feeling like an intruder, he knocked on the door. There was no answer, so he twisted the doorknob—and it opened easily.

She was gone. A fast search through the room revealed her luggage was gone as well. Matthew slumped against the doorframe, the lamp wavering in his hand, flabbergasted to realize she had cleared out her belongings. Where could she be at this hour?

Had she run away? If so, where? The town of Pierce was small, and to the best of his knowledge he was the only church member residing in town. Everyone else lived out in the settlement, including the Yoders. The only *Englischer* she knew was Lucy Naylor. Could she be staying with the older couple? He didn't know where the Naylors lived.

Matthew blinked back tears. He had managed to chase a pregnant woman out into the cold night, a woman who'd thought she could trust him and depend upon him. *"Schtupid, schtupid,"* he muttered to himself.

Slowly descending the stairs, he realized how much he looked forward to seeing her at all times. Could he really overlook her pregnancy? He honestly didn't know. But one thing he *did* know: he had to find her.

He set the lamp on the front desk and saw something he had overlooked before: her room key. Picking it up, he held it in his hand for a moment, trying to think clearly.

She had four suitcases containing all her worldly possessions. If she had gone to Lucy's house, how had she transported them? Had she used the telephone to call the older woman?

Unless…

Matthew snatched up the lamp and went into the laundry room, where he normally kept two luggage carts. One was missing.

That meant she had loaded her suitcases on it and used the cart to transport her belongings elsewhere. While he didn't know where Lucy Naylor lived, he was certain Cara hadn't dragged a luggage cart halfway across town.

In that case, the only other place she could possibly be was the cannery. He knew she had a door key to the seldom-used street door of that space. Could she be bunking down there for the night?

Without further ado, he grabbed his own keys, locked the boardinghouse door behind him and strode off into the night.

Chapter Sixteen

Cara had never been inside the cannery after-hours. After pulling the luggage cart inside after her, she locked the door and turned to face the dark, echoing space. Somehow it seemed larger, eerier than when she was here for work.

There was a light switch near the door, but Cara didn't want to advertise her presence by turning on the electric lights. The interior was lit faintly by the glow of the outside streetlights. She groped her way through the bakery area toward the cannery side of the room at the far end, and pulled out the oil lamp she kept there as an emergency light. Within a few moments she had it lit.

It was cold in the room. Cara blessed the Yoders for their foresight in installing the woodstove. She crumpled some newspapers and stuffed them into the stove's firebox, laid some kindling on top and struck a match. Within a few minutes, the stove started to heat up. Cara lingered nearby, holding out her hands to the warmth, drawing comfort from the cheerful flicker of the flames through the glass windows of the stove.

She removed her cloak and started to hang it on a hook, then thought the better of it. The cloak would act as a blanket for the night. She eyed the comfortable padded chairs she and Matthew had selected some time ago. The cannery was no place to spend the night. It wasn't designed for it, after all. But being here was better than being at the boardinghouse, and facing Matthew's derision.

Over and over she replayed his words

in her mind. *It's over, Cara. It's over.* She had deceived him from the start, lied by omission about her condition, and fully understood his reaction.

She understood, yes. But understanding his anger didn't make it any easier to cope with losing him.

She pulled the luggage cart over to the carpeted area where the chairs were located, and opened one case to find her hairbrush. She removed her *kapp*, unpinned her hair and brushed it out. Then she rebraided the long tresses into a single thick plait down her back. She would be sleeping in her dress and apron as it was. She had no intention of sleeping with her *kapp* on.

The sight of the *kapp* sitting by itself on a chair made her remember its purpose. It was a prayer covering. Women were supposed to wear them to keep them prepared to pray at any time. Cara sat down on another chair and stared at the *kapp*. Slowly she reached over and lifted it up, then replaced it over her braided hair. She needed to pray.

She prayed for guidance. She prayed for wisdom. She prayed for direction. And all the time, she tried to ignore the aching, empty space inside her where Matthew's presence had been.

Was she a fool for falling in love with him? She wasn't sure. Unquestionably she had been viewing him as a convenient solution to her problem. She'd hoped he would be a provider, a protector and, yes, a father to her babies—both the one she was currently expecting, and any future children they might have. In short, she hoped he would be all the things married men in the church were as a matter of course for their wives…with one exception. Becoming a father to another man's baby was a lot to ask of anyone.

A small part of her looked at her hopes and dreams with scorn. She realized she *had* expected Matthew to be her white knight, riding to the rescue and marrying

her despite her pregnancy. At an uncon-
scious level, she'd hoped he would offer
her baby a name and take away her own
shame.

But if she had she told him from the
beginning that she was pregnant, everything would be different. She may never
have been invited to travel to Montana
to begin with. Nor would she have seen
Matthew's goodness and loyalty. It was
that side of him she had fallen in love
with.

But this new Matthew—the furious
one, the one who told her it was over between them—that was a side she had
never seen before. Now she must be prepared to stand alone.

She sighed, removed her *kapp* once
again and rummaged until she found her
toothbrush. She washed up in the cannery's bathroom, stoked the woodstove
with another log or two, and settled into
one of the wingback chairs, exhausted
by the evening's emotion. She pulled her

cloak over herself like a blanket and prepared to spend an uncomfortable night.

But barely had she started to doze when
she heard a banging on the street door.
Cara jumped to her feet, her heart thump-
ing. She knew who it was even before
she tiptoed over to the darkened window.
Peering out, she saw Matthew, his face
like a thundercloud.

Cara leaned against the door, a hand
pressed to her chest, and took deep
breaths. *Stay calm, stay calm*, she thought.

She unlocked the door and confronted
him warily.

"What nonsense is this?" he growled.
"Spending the night in the cannery?"

She lifted her chin. "I knew I wasn't
wanted in the boardinghouse anymore. I
no longer have a right to trespass on your
hospitality."

"Cara, *du bist ein idiot. Heimkommen.*"

She drew herself. "I'm *not* being an
idiot," she retorted. "And I'm *not* coming home. You told me yourself it's over.

I knew I wasn't welcome anymore. What else did you expect me to do?"

He ran a hand over his face. "I said a lot of things I regret. Cara, *bitte. Komm* back with me."

Her wariness increased. Her emotions had been yanked every which way today. She wasn't sure she could take much more. "Why?" she inquired with some sarcasm. "So you can toss me out again?"

He glared at her. "I didn't toss you out. You left. You're being ridiculous, running to the cannery as if you expect you could stay here indefinitely."

Cara had a choice. She could either spend an uncomfortable night sleeping in a chair in the cannery, clinging to her pathetic dignity while she made desperate and unthinkable plans for her future prospects; or she could return to the boarding-house with Matthew and hash out their issues. She sighed. It wasn't much of a choice, really. "Let me get my things."

All her suitcases but one were still

stacked on the luggage cart. Cara gathered up her toiletries and stuffed them back in the partially unzipped valise, then lifted it back on the cart. She snatched her *kapp* and plopped it, unpinned, over her braided hair, recognizing how ridiculous it must look when worn so improperly. Then she swung her cloak over her shoulders.

During the moments it took her to gather her things, she noticed Matthew glancing around at the bakery space with an assessing look on his face. But he didn't say anything. He merely took the luggage cart and rolled it toward the door.

The night had gotten colder. She walked beside him along the quiet streets illuminated by streetlights. An occasional car passed. They crossed Main Street and went down the darker side street where the boardinghouse loomed, large and black, dominating one block.

"I had to get the spare key from the stable," he said as he unlocked the door.

"Ach," she replied, startled. "It didn't occur to me I'd be locking you out."

"Well, I did leave in something of a huff."

In the dim glow of the courtyard, she caught a gleam of humor in his eyes. It gave her hope.

However, she said nothing as he held the door for her, then pulled the luggage cart behind him into the lobby area.

"I found your room key," he said as he parked the cart near the base of the stairs. "But not until after I'd been up to your room and determined you'd left. I can't tell you how much it tied me up in knots."

"Just as I can't tell you how much I was tied in knots when *you* left," she retorted. She stopped herself from admitting just how deep her despair had sunk during those first few minutes alone in the boardinghouse. "Where did you go?"

"To talk to the bishop." He led the way behind the check-in desk and opened the door to his private quarters.

"I see. So now he knows I'm pregnant?"

"*Ja*, he does."

"And I suppose I'll be expecting a meeting with him soon enough, asking me to leave the church?"

Matthew whirled. "What?"

"You heard me."

"Cara, you know the bishop would never ask something like that."

"Well, my father would. Why not another man in authority?"

He scowled. "Your father is not a church leader. For *gut* reason, evidently."

"Fair enough. But why did you have to tell the bishop?"

"How much longer do you think you could have kept it a secret?"

She had no answer. Instead, she sighed. "I'm so tired…" She turned and sank down on the living room sofa in front of a coffee table.

"I'm making tea." Matthew rekindled the glowing coals in the woodstove and put a kettle on.

Cara watched him bustle around the kitchen, preparing two mugs. He knew exactly how she liked her tea. She said nothing while he worked, but she observed his impassive face and neutral expression. Her mind felt almost detached, skimming along on the surface, not knowing how the anticipated conversation would end.

One thing Matthew had not done since fetching her back from the cannery was profess his undying love and promise to live happily ever after with her. That alone made her expect the worst.

At last he placed a mug on the coffee table in front her and took his own mug. He sat down opposite. "Three weeks from now is Saturday, November eighteenth," he said. "How do you feel about that as a wedding date?"

Matthew watched the utter shock on Cara's face. Her face drained of color, and she stared at him, speechless.

A few moments of silence went by.

Finally she started sputtering. "But… but…you said…"

"I said a lot of things," he replied. "I was furious. But the bishop—and his wife—managed to knock a little sense into me. I won't deny I was shocked. But of the many things the bishop said, one thing stands out."

She pinched the bridge of her nose in a gesture of weariness. "And what was that?"

"He said, while your pregnancy changes the immediate future, it doesn't change *you*. You're same person I fell in love with."

Her eyes grew wide as she stared at him. "You love me?"

"*Ja.* Now the question is, do you still want to get married?"

"*J-ja,*" she stuttered.

"Then the next question—or perhaps it should have been the previous question— is do you love me?"

"Matthew, I've loved you almost before I met you."

He was reassured when she spoke without hesitation.

"Then let's get married," he said. "We'll make it work."

Without warning, she broke down weeping. This time he had no reluctance in leaping up from his chair and sitting down next to her. He pulled her against his chest and simply let her cry. Her unfastened *kapp* fell to the floor, but he made no move to pick it up. Right now there were more important things he had to do, such as to comfort his future wife.

She garbled some incoherent words he couldn't understand. He fished in his pocket and found a handkerchief, which he handed over to her, and waited for the storm to pass.

But it didn't. Instead he listened as she poured out her self-loathing. "I—I thought Andrew and I would be together forever," she sobbed. "So I gave away the special thing I w-would have been able to offer my *hutband* on our wedding n-night. I should have known better..."

Matthew found himself murmuring words in an attempt to soothe her. "I can't change the past," he said. "But I can change your future. The bishop made it clear to me that you and the baby are a package deal. Cara, I'll be honest—up until I saw you standing in the cannery door a little while ago, I wasn't certain getting married was right for me. But I'm certain now. I think *Gott* put it on me that you should be my *frau*, and your baby will be my *kinder*."

At last the storm of tears abated and Cara lay slumped across his chest. He suspected she was exhausted after the emotional roller coaster of the day. This suspicion was confirmed when he realized she had, incredibly, fallen asleep. Her dark lashes created a half circle against her cheeks, her breathing grew deep and even, and she gave a little sigh.

He couldn't move without waking her. He didn't *want* to move. Stealthily he drew a throw pillow toward him and put it behind his neck, and leaned his head back. It felt wonderful to hold her in his arms, even though the reasons had been emotionally harrowing.

And then he, too, fell asleep.

Cara opened her eyes, confused. An early predawn light vaguely lit up the room. She was positioned funny. Where was she? Why wasn't she in bed? She moved her head a fraction and realized she was in Matthew's arms. He was sound asleep, his head resting on a throw pillow, his arms locked around her. They were seated on the sofa in the living room.

In a moment it all came flooding back—confessing her pregnancy, his furious anger, his storming away, her departure to the cannery, coming back to the boardinghouse…

And she was almost certain he had proposed marriage to her. Not next year, but this year. In three weeks, in fact. Or was it a dream?

She passed a hand over her face, and the motion woke Matthew. He smacked his lips and peered down at her with bleary eyes. *"Guder mariye,"* he mumbled.

"Guder mariye," she replied. She drew herself out of his arms and stretched out the kinks from sleeping in such a cramped position. "So how much of last night was a bad dream?"

"Most of it, I would say." He scrubbed both hands over his face. "But it doesn't mean it didn't all happen."

"Hmm." Cara got off the sofa and went to splash water on her face in the bathroom. She came back to find Matthew doing the same thing at the kitchen sink. He snatched up a towel to wipe his face.

The room was chilly. Cara opened the firebox door to the woodstove and peered at the cold ashes, then started crumpling newspapers to start a fire.

By unspoken consensus, they didn't say much while they put themselves and the kitchen to rights. But within half an hour, each had a hot mug of tea in their hands and sat down at the kitchen table.

"So it wasn't a dream." Cara spooned a bit of sugar into her tea and stirred.

"*Nein.* Particularly the part about getting married in three weeks."

She felt herself blush. "Matthew, are you sure?"

"*Ja*, I'm sure. Cara, I'm ashamed of my reaction to your condition. It was my pride and ego that was hurt more than anything else. The bishop made it clear last night that the only way I could cast stones is if I was without sin—which clearly I'm not. Lois also handed me my head when I complained about you not telling me sooner," he added in a rueful tone. "She explained what happens with pregnant women and hormones, and how that can impact making decisions."

"*Gott segne* Lois," muttered Cara,

blessing the woman and making a mental note to thank the bishop's wife next time she saw her. "What else did they say?"

Matthew exhaled and quirked a smile at her. "What *didn't* they say?" he responded. "They helped me understand how much I loved you. In fact, Lois asked me the one question that helped clear my head. She said, shock and dismay aside, what are my feelings for you? That's when I realized how much you meant to me."

"But…" Cara was determined to be fair. "Married in three weeks? Wouldn't you rather wait another year?"

"Why? It will be tough enough for you having a baby. It will be tougher having it on your own as a single woman. We'll get married, Cara, and then *we'll* have a baby, not just you."

She blinked back tears. "It's more than I'd hoped for, Matthew. I still feel shame for coming into a marriage with another man's child, but…"

"What's done is done," he interrupted again.

"I could still give the baby up for adoption—"

"*Nein.* Absolutely not. That's another thing the bishop told me—that if I request you put the baby up for adoption as a condition for getting married, you might do it, but you would resent me the rest of your life. To be honest, at no point did that ever occur to me. I want to make that clear."

With her hands wrapped around the mug, Cara closed her eyes. She didn't have her *kapp* on, but she prayed anyway and hoped *Gott* would hear her. *"Danke,"* she prayed simply. *"Vielen dank, Gott."*

She opened her eyes and looked at the noble man sitting opposite her. His clothing was crumpled, his face a bit puffy from a bad night's sleep…and she thought he never looked more handsome than he was now. Her heart swelled with love.

But then an unwelcome thought occurred to her. "What about your parents?"

His face darkened and hardened. "They'll be dismayed," he admitted, and related the reason behind his uncle's life-long bachelorhood as the source for their opposition to a mail-order bride. "I sometimes wonder what might have happened if Uncle Micah *had* married that woman," he said. "Would they have been happy? I don't know. But what you don't know is this—we won't be homeless. Even if my parents turn us out of the boardinghouse, we won't be living in a motel. Abe Yoder knew my *daed* was dead set against a mail-order bride, so he said I could fix up the bakery area for living quarters if necessary."

"I just hate being the cause of a rift between you and your parents."

"What my parents sometimes forget is I'm a grown man. I have the backing of the bishop on this. You won't be ostracized by the community if Samuel and Lois Beiler are behind us."

She laid her hands palm up on the table, and was gratified when he covered them with his own. "Matthew, I'll make you a promise. If we marry, and if you become the father of this baby, I promise you to be the best possible wife you could ever hope for."

His hands tightened over hers. "I guess we should start picking names."

Cara knew she had one more thing to do…and she had no intention of telling Matthew before she did it.

Epilogue

The Yoders' store was crowded. Cara and Lucy Naylor wheeled a loaded cart of peach salsa out of the cannery and prepared to restock the shelves. The item had become a general favorite in town, and it sold almost as fast as Cara and Lucy could make it.

"Where's Matthew today?" asked the older woman, transferring jars from the cart to a shelf.

"He had...an errand," hedged Cara, smiling to herself.

"It's a good thing he installed that half-wall around the cannery, otherwise we'd have people underfoot among all the equipment," remarked Lucy. "As it is, we've been answering more and more questions from people about food preservation."

Cara smiled at her assistant. Lucy had proved to be an invaluable employee, enthusiastic and diligent, and she blessed the day the Yoders hired her.

Without warning, the pain came again. Cara paused and leaned against the cart, closing her eyes. She could feel the changes taking place in her body as her child prepared to enter the world.

"You're starting to make me nervous." Lucy looked at her critically. "You look like you're going to burst at any moment."

The pain retreated, and Cara straightened up and ran a hand over her extended midsection. "Shall I tell you a secret? I'm already in early labor."

Lucy's eyes widened and a look of panic spread on her face. "What? You're in labor and you're still working? Oh my, go sit down! Should I call an ambulance?"

Cara chuckled. "Calm down! That's why Matthew isn't here. He's already on his way to let the midwife know. I have plenty of time, and I suspect Miriam—she's the midwife—won't be here right away. But I'm just so grateful you're able to run the cannery on your own now."

"I had a feeling it's why you were determined to make sure I was trained and ready to work alone so quickly."

"*Ja*, that's exactly right."

"Where is Colin?"

"Matthew took him to stay with his parents. They insisted. It's hard to believe Colin is already two years old. I sometimes wonder who loves that boy more—Matthew or his *daed*."

"Matthew," answered Lucy promptly. "And since you got married several months before Colin was even born, that doesn't surprise me."

"He's never fallen down on his promise to treat Colin as his own."

"And it's easy to tell you've never fallen down on your promise to be the best wife you can be to Matthew."

Cara chuckled. "That wasn't a hard promise to keep, trust me." She caught her breath as another pain started. They were still mild, but she knew what she needed to do. "I think I'd better head home," she said.

"Yes," said Lucy briskly. "The customers don't need to see you having a baby right here." She gave Cara a hug. "I'll handle things until you're back on your feet again."

"*Danke.*" She returned the older woman's hug. It would likely be many days before she set foot inside the cannery, and weeks before she could resume a regular attendance. However, Lucy had proved to be so competent that Cara had no qualms leaving her in charge.

Cara walked over to where Mabel

Yoder was ringing up a customer at the cash register. Cara waited until her boss was free.

"I'm off," she said, smiling and resting a hand on her midsection. "This little one is anxious to be born."

"I knew you didn't have much time. Do you want Abe to drive you back to the boardinghouse?"

"*Nein*, but *danke*. Matthew took Colin to stay with his parents, and he'll bring Miriam back with him. It's early yet, and I suspect the baby won't be born until after midnight or so."

Mabel chuckled. "Then she'll mostly be twiddling her thumbs until your labor is further advanced."

"That's okay. She'll have her hands busy keeping Matthew from worrying himself to death. He was the same way when Colin was born." Cara smiled at the thought of her husband's anxious preparation for fatherhood. "I told him it wasn't necessary to get Miriam so early, but he insisted."

"I'm so happy for you, Cara." Mabel spoke softly. "I know you both had a rough start to your marriage, but I don't think I've ever seen two people so much in love."

"Ja." It wasn't common for people to touch on such personal issues, but Mabel had become a good friend. *"Gott* knew what He was doing in bringing us together. It's been two years and we've become *gut* friends in addition to *hutband* and wife. I never knew a marriage could be this way."

A bell over the door jingled, and Cara looked over to see Matthew enter. As always, her heart leaped at the sight of him. He looked a bit disheveled and out of breath as he dashed over to her. "Are you okay?" he asked anxiously. "Do I need to carry you?"

She chuckled. "Wouldn't that be a sight? I'm fine. That is… I will be in a moment." She closed her eyes and leaned on the cash register counter. She felt Matthew's arms encircle her, comforting her as the pain built and then ebbed.

"Miriam's in the buggy," he told her. "Should I go get her?"

"Nein." Cara took a deep breath and straightened up. She gave her husband a lopsided grin. "But it's time to go, I think."

"I'll pray," offered Mabel.

Matthew threw his arm around her thickened waist, bracing her as they walked toward the door. "You know what I was thinking a few minutes ago?" he asked.

"What?"

"How you had the courage of a lion when you went to talk to my parents two years ago, before the wedding. All by yourself and without me knowing. You completely brought them around, and they've loved you like a daughter ever since. And Colin—he's as much their grandchild as any of my sister's *kinner*."

"Your parents didn't need a lot of convincing," she told him. "They're *gut* and generous people."

His arm tightened around her waist as he opened the door for her. *"Komm,"* he said. "Let's go bring our second child into the world."

* * * * *

Dear Reader,

The year was 1990. My husband and I were newlyweds. In the backyard of our rental house, I planted two tomato plants. I don't know what was in the soil of that mini garden, but I ended up with more tomatoes than I knew what to do with. Vaguely in the back of my mind I remember hearing about a food-preservation technique called canning, but I knew nothing about it.

So I set out to learn. And when I pulled those first ruby-red jars of tomatoes out of the pot of boiling water and set them on a towel to cool, I realized one very important thing: I was hooked. I mean, I was *seriously* hooked.

Thirty-five years and thousands of jars of home-canned food later, I freely admit to being addicted to canning. The pantry my husband built me remains my pride and joy. There's a lot of my husband in the character of Matthew.

I hope you enjoyed the story of Cara and Matthew. I love hearing from readers, so feel free to email me at patricelewis@protonmail.com.

Blessings,
Patrice